AMANTE

One of the Four Heavenly Kings of the Libere Rebellion, a group opposed to Masato's party. She's a loose-lipped Magic Fencer prone to blabbing critical information.

"I am one of the Four Heavenly Kings of the Libere Rebellion. We reject the concept of mothers. I am Anti-Mom Amante. Not that there's any rule saying you have to give your name to a total stranger. Is there?"

"Hey, Master, if you want something, just spit it out! How 'bout that?"

"Um, um... Master! Please leave everything to me!"

WISE

Tragically useless high school Sage whose magic is always sealed.

PORTA

A twelve-year-old Traveling Merchant treasured for her ability to soothe the party members' hearts.

"Master,
I await your
instructions."

MEDHI

Seems like your classic heroine,
but this high school Cleric harbors
a certain darkness within.

"What else?
A little mom service...in bed!"

CONTENTS

Dachima Inaka

Do You
Love Your
MOM
and Her Two-Hit
Multi-Target
Attacks
?

VOLUME 3

DACHIMA INAKA

Illustration by IIDA POCHI.

YEN
ON

New York

Do You Love Your Mom and Her Two-Hit Multi-Target Attacks?, Vol. 3

▶ Dachima Inaka

▶ Translation by Andrew Cunningham

▶ Cover art by Iida Pochi.

This book is a work of fiction. Names, characters, places, and incidents are the product of the author's imagination or are used fictitiously. Any resemblance to actual events, locales, or persons, living or dead, is coincidental.

TSUJO KOGEKI GA ZENTAI KOGEKI DE 2KAI KOGEKI NO OKASAN WA SUKI DESUKA? Vol.3
©Dachima Inaka, Iida Pochi. 2017
First published in Japan in 2017 by KADOKAWA CORPORATION, Tokyo.
English translation rights arranged with KADOKAWA CORPORATION, Tokyo
through TUTTLE-MORI AGENCY, INC., Tokyo.

English translation © 2019 by Yen Press, LLC

First Yen On Edition: July 2019

Yen On is an imprint of Yen Press, LLC.
The Yen On name and logo are trademarks of Yen Press, LLC.

The publisher is not responsible for websites (or their content) that are not owned by the publisher.

Library of Congress Cataloging-in-Publication Data
Names: Inaka, Dachima, author. | Pochi., Iida, illustrator. |
    Cunningham, Andrew, 1979– translator.
Title: Do you love your mom and her two-hit multi-target attacks? /
    Dachima Inaka ; illustration by Iida Pochi ; translation by
    Andrew Cunningham.
Other titles: Tsujo kogeki ga zentai kogeki de 2kai kogeki no
    okasan wa suki desuka?. English
Description: First Yen On edition. | New York : Yen On, 2018–
Identifiers: LCCN 2018030739 | ISBN 9781975328009 (v. 1 : pbk.) |
    ISBN 9781975328375 (v. 2 : pbk.) | ISBN 9781975328399 (v. 3 : pbk.)
Subjects: LCSH: Virtual reality—Fiction.
Classification: LCC PL871.5.N35 T7813 2018 | DDC 895.63/6—dc23
LC record available at https://lccn.loc.gov/2018030739

ISBNs: 978-1-9753-2839-9 (paperback)
        978-1-9753-2840-5 (ebook)

10 9 8 7 6 5 4 3 2 1

LSC-C

Printed in the United States of America

▶ Yen On
150 West 30th Street, 19th Floor
New York, NY 10001

▶ Visit us at yenpress.com
facebook.com/yenpress
twitter.com/yenpress
yenpress.tumblr.com
instagram.com/yenpress

Prologue   A Certain Mom's Progress Report

Have you gotten closer to your son or daughter?
I Feel The Gap Between Us Is Closing Little By Little.
Have you had more opportunities to talk to your son or daughter?
Quite A Lot More Than We Did At Home. I'm Delighted.
Has your son or daughter said anything that made you happy?
I Was So Glad When He Said, "Yeah, My Mom's The Best."
Has your son or daughter said anything that made you unhappy?
Nothing, Really. (Although There Were A Few Things He Said That Made Me Sad Or Lonely.)
Where have you gone with your son or daughter?
Different Cities And Towns, A School, And Some Fields, Too!
Have you learned what your son or daughter likes?
I Suspected It All Along, But It Seems Like He Definitely Loves Me.
Have you learned what your son or daughter dislikes?
He Especially Seems To Have It In For Monsters That Do Strange Things To Me.
What are your son's or daughter's strong points?
Everything.
What are your son's or daughter's weak points?
If I Must Put Something, I Suppose He Can Be A Little Rude.
How is your adventure with your son or daughter going?
Every Day Is A Delight. I Would Recommended This Experience To Anyone.
(Optional) If there are any products or elements you'd like to see added to the game, please list them here. These will assist us with future development.
I Think It Would Be Lovely If There Were Digital Cameras. I Would Love A Way To Preserve My Son's Actions Forever. It Also Seems Like My Son And His Friends Sometimes Really Miss Cheap Snacks, So I Think You Should Add Convenience Stores To The Towns.

She finished filling out the survey.

"Well, that's that. I hope that's what they're looking for..."

Mamako was staring at the pop-up window screen, her head tilted to one side.

The survey was about the mystery-technology-fueled full-dive MMORPG known only *MMMMMORPG* (working title), played by pairs consisting of one parent and one child. The results were being collected by the Japanese government, who ran the game, so it would never do to rush through them.

Was this good enough? Mamako checked over her entries again. As she did...

"Now! Hah! And for the finish! Highest Sky-Save! Gooooooo! Splat! ...Heh, nailed it."

...she heard her beloved son shouting. She glanced that way and saw Masato in the yard behind the inn. He seemed to be doing some sort of sword training. It happened to include dramatic posing after every attack. He was really getting into it.

She didn't want to interrupt, but she also felt like this was the perfect place to ask her beloved son's advice, so Mamako called out, "Hey, Ma-kun! Do you have a minute? I have a favor to—"

"Auuuughhh!! M-M-M-Mom?! Since when are you...? Have you been there the whole time?!"

"Mm? Y-yes, I have... Why is that such a surprise?"

"It...it isn't!! I'm not in the least bit surprised just because I thought I was alone and practicing my original (mega-cool) ultimate move, yet it turns out you were watching me the whole time!! ...So, uh, wh-what is it? Let's get this over with!"

"R-right... Well, to be honest, the government sent me this survey, so I filled it out, but...I'm just not sure about the whole thing. I was hoping you'd check it over for me. Do you mind?"

"Check a survey for you? ...Is that it? Geez... Okay, sure, whatever."

Making a big show of reluctance, Masato abandoned his training and came over to Mamako. The sweat glistening on his brow was awe-inspiring and secured his place as the world's coolest son (in Mamako's highly subjective opinion).

If she called out to him, he answered. If she asked him for a favor, he said yes. This alone made Mamako highly emotional, and her joy overflowed into a beaming smile.

Meanwhile, Masato glanced over the survey entries and scowled. Embarrassment and anger left him beet red.

"Mooooooooom?! What the hell is this?! You just wrote a bunch of lies!"

"Huh? But everything I wrote is the truth!"

"It is not! When did I ever say, 'Yeah, my mom's the best'?! That's a blatant and utter lie!"

"Oh my… Perhaps that was a bit of wishful thinking…"

"This is an official government survey, so take it seriously! And why are you capitalizing every single word?! Gah, I can't take it! Please just fix this! For the sake of my sanity!"

"A-all right, I'll fix it. Now, where is that EDIT button? …Oh, is this it?" Mamako absently pressed the SUBMIT button. The survey was successfully submitted.

Masato just gave her a look.

"Why'd you just…submit it like that…? Don't just hit random buttons, pleeeease…"

"O-oh? …Gosh! Mommy can be such a ditzy little thing sometimes! Tee-hee!" She stuck her tongue out.

"I told you never to do that! And you're not little, either! Arghh! Arghhh! ARGHHHHHHHHHHHHHHHHHHHHHHHHHHHHHHHHH!!"

What her son needed was not levels or skills but endurance.

Once again, their family adventure was off to a great start.

Chapter 1   Whoa, There's a Rut Here. Not Stepping in That. Definitely Not.

Picture a hero's magnificent battle in your mind and act accordingly.

You're passionate yet clearheaded.

You release your physical tension and bend your knees slightly, lowering your center of gravity.

Firm grip on the Holy Sword Firmamento, blessed with the power of the heavens. Cast aside your fears and step forward.

"Riiiiiight! Let's do thiiiiiis!"

With that forceful cry, the hero Masato charged, closing the gap between him and his foes…

And as he did, with flawless timing, support from the rear arrived.

"I'll back you up! …*Spara la magia per mirare… Salire!*"

One of his companions, the pure white Cleric Medhi, cast a support spell that buffed his attack. She raised her staff high, and a powerful light shot out of it and poured down onto Masato.

As an expert in recovery and support magic, Medhi's spell was highly effective. Masato received a substantial physical boost. Confident that he could beat anything, he put everything he had into a single blow. Time for Masato's attack.

A bold swing from above, followed by a *splaaaat!*

"Yes! A critical hit! My attack defeated it…!"

At least, he thought it had. Masato had been sure of it.

"Not yet! There are still more enemies!"

Racing up from behind him, the crimson Sage Wise nimbly stepped to the fore with a magic tome open in one hand, ready to attack.

"The enemy is a land monster! Masato's attacks are specialized for anti-air and proved ineffective! My chain cast magic will finish it off!"

"Hey, Wise! Do you really need to dual-cast in order to finish it off?"

"I do! Why? Because I want to!"

"Okay, got it, suit yourself."

"I always do! I'm so amazing that my amazing chain cast will blow these enemies away! *Spara la magia per mirare... Vento Taglio!* And! *Bomba Fiamma!*"

Wise's chain cast activated. A set of wind blades sliced their target apart, and then the pieces burst into flames.

When the roaring flames subsided, there was nothing left but cinders.

Masato's party defeated the monsters! Their overwhelming strength led to yet another victory! Well done!

This was definitely how it was supposed to be.

"All right, that's pretty much the basic idea. Flawless teamwork."

"Yes, I think we're more or less in sync now."

"No enemy can stand against us now! Mwa-ha-ha."

They put their weapons away, grinning at one another as if pleased with their performance.

Except the enemy had been entirely imaginary. This was just practice.

With the Cleric Medhi newly added to their party, their overall effectiveness had dramatically improved. The key to this was to find ways to make their individual skills work together. Only when all parts were working in harmony was the party's true strength unleashed. Hence, practice.

The results were pretty good. Wise was getting carried away, and the smug look on her face was a little annoying, but, well, she did have what you might consider a cute face to begin with. Then there was Medhi and her phenomenal beauty, smiling elegantly... Looking at the two of them put a smile on Masato's face, too.

"...Heh-heh. Man, what a trip."

"Wait, Masato, what are you smirking about? Creep."

"Wiiiise! Stop calling me a creep! I was being all happy to have such reliable companions! Technically."

"Oh, right, right, *such* an honor to be in your party."

Masato and Wise started bickering like always, and then Medhi effortlessly joined in.

"Hee-hee... You should really just admit it, Wise. I feel the same way as Masato. Having reliable companions is truly a blessing."

"Yeah, Medhi's right. Being able to share in your feelings is what friendship's all about... But since you don't seem capable of doing that, then I've got no choice but to kick you ou—"

"D-don't do that! I agree, obviously! Myself included, we're definitely a good party. Emphasis on the 'myself included.'"

"Very true. The three of us form a magnificent party...if it was just the three of us."

Medhi glanced meaningfully to one side.

"Mm, yeah." Wise followed her gaze, clearly conscious of the same thing.

Masato himself preferred not to look. But the unshakable reality wouldn't change whether he looked or not, so he gave up and followed her gaze, too.

All three of them were, of course, looking at the same person.

"Hee-hee-hee! Mommy will do her best, too!"

So youthful that if she claimed to have a son in high school, no one would believe her.

Flaxen hair, her favorite dress, an easygoing air.

The only mom with two-hit multi-target attacks—Mamako.

But if this had been actual combat... Well, look! A hoard of monsters loom over her!

"Here's Mommy's attack! *Hyah!*"

In her right hand, the Holy Sword of Mother Earth, Terra di Madre. In her left, the Holy Sword of Mother Ocean, Altura. Both blades swung.

A moment later, countless jagged rock spikes shot out of the earth, and at the same time countless water bullets fired. The looming monsters are run through or riddled with holes, leaving none behind.

She made it look easy. Battles were over in seconds.

And after the battles, it was time for the littlest one—their hardest worker.

When monsters are defeated, they leave dice-shaped objects behind known as gems. These could be exchanged for money, and it was the job of a twelve-year-old Traveling Merchant named Porta to collect them.

"Wow! So many gems! This is well worth gathering! Great work!"

Porta opened up her magic shoulder bag and used both hands to scoop the gems into it. Like a bulldozer. No, that makes it sound imposing. This was cuter. Let's call it the Portadozer. The world's first dozer so cute you wanted to put it on your lap and pet it.

Then Porta looked up in alarm.

"...Oh! More monsters! Careful!"

Monsters sighted. Prepare for battle!

Time to show the results of their combo practice. Masato, Wise, and Medhi all stopped watching Porta and turned, ready to run to the battlefield... Except...

Before they even had a chance to take a single step...

"Don't worry! Leave it to Mommy! *Hyah!*"

...Mamako attacked. Her two AOE attacks might split damage among all targets, but even with this many monsters, that was still enough raw damage to carve right through them. Instant death.

As always, combat was over before it began. "Yay! I did it!" Mamako hopped up and down happily, and Porta dashed over to start collecting.

Meanwhile...

Masato, Wise, and Medhi, poised to run, slowly reverted to standing posture.

They stared at one another in silence. Looking at one another did them no good, but what choice did they have?

Medhi spoke first. "...Um, may I ask something?"

"Yeah. If you have anything to say, please do. We promise to listen." Masato smiled.

"The two of us have walked this path before. No need to hold anything back." Wise smiled as well.

"Um, I just wanted to say... This party's combat works quite different from how I had imagined it. Is it always like this?"

"More or less. Combat pretty much always starts with Mom's carpet bombing. And ends with it."

"So opportunities for a healer like me to use support magic to give us an edge in combat are...?"

"Not gonna happen in any normal fight. In a boss fight... Well, every now and then, I guess."

"Th-then using recovery magic to heal injured party members..."

"Like I said, the carpet bombing always ends the fight, so nobody ever gets hurt."

"Th-then what should I do in combat?"

"The same thing we just did."

Stand perfectly still and watch Mamako's attacks go off. The end.

If having nothing to do ever got to them, the useless members could work together and practice their combos, making themselves feel like they were doing something. There was always that option.

But basically, they had nothing to do.

Masato and Wise both gave her bleak smiles, so Medhi stared at her feet.

"...If you'll pardon me," she said and walked away. She stopped by a boulder at the side of the road and glared at it.

The darkness within Medhi began to leak out.

"...*Sigh*... It's not like I want to go and yell at Mamako or anything," she muttered. "That's not it. That isn't it, but even so... What do I do with this frustration?! I'm a healer. I want to be useful in combat. I want to secure my place in the party... Argghh... This is so depressing..."

As she mumbled to herself, Medhi began kicking the boulder. She used the flat of her foot—the infamous yakuza kick. Then she smacked it with her staff. Medhi was a Melee Healer specializing in bash damage and putting quite a lot of force into this. It was extremely frightening. Like a shroud of darkness had surrounded her despite the cloudless blue sky overhead.

As a result of a stressful upbringing under an emotionally abusive mother, Medhi had a lot of repressed negative energy. Accumulated over many years, it was not so easily expelled. Even now that she and her mother had reached something of an understanding, this side of her still remained, and the negative energy had become her dark power. At the moment, they had found no cure. Hence, boulder abuse.

It certainly was an alarming aspect of her personality that Masato would prefer not to see, but...

"*Sigh*... I know just how she feels. I was pretty much the same early on. Every time Mom jumped out ahead of me, I'd get all mad."

"Yeah. Thinking back, I used to do the same thing. I got so stressed about not being able to do anything… Now I'm just used to it…"

Wise sounded almost like she'd accepted the situation. But a moment later, she shook her head.

"Look, Masato. Maybe we've given up on it all…but I feel like that's not a good thing."

Masato nodded.

"Yeah… Things have to change. We have to change. We've gotta get stronger… Stronger than any enemy. Stronger than Mom."

Masato felt like he was desperately pumping at a well that had run dry.

Meanwhile, Wise just burst out laughing.

"Pfft! 'We've gotta get stronger'! You looked *sooo* serious when you said that just now! I guess there really are boys who talk like that! That was hilarious! I'm dying!"

"W-wait… Did you just bait me into that?!"

"I can't believe you fell for it again! You're such an idiot! …Hang on, didn't you just say something like that the other day and then totally self-destructed? And then Mamako ended up doing everything… Oh, wait, is this déjà vu? Are you about to self-destruct again? Wow, I can't wait!"

"There's nothing to wait for! What's your problem anyway? You're the worst. Just for the record, this time it'll be different! This won't end up like last time!"

Yes. This time would be different. He swore it would be.

This time, Masato would get the strength he desired! No matter what!

Probably!

And so.

"Well, everyone, let's—"

"Let's go! Come on! Woo!"

""""Woo!""""

"Hey, Mom! I was about to say… Oh, never mind. I'm done being a whiny brat who complains about that every time. It's fine. But I just…

think nobody would be at all upset if you'd put a little consideration into letting the party's hero be the leader sometimes… But whatever, it's fine."

Masato was talking, but nobody was listening.

Now that Mamako had polished off all monsters in the area, she led the party away. They took a leisurely stroll across the field with her up in front.

A mother, two fifteen-year-old girls, and one twelve-year-old girl all chattering away. Masato was reluctant to join in and felt it wasn't actually an option at all, so he voluntarily chose to bring up the rear, trailing along behind them.

Gazing absently at their backs, a thought struck him.

I could've been a harem MC surrounded by women. That was a possibility once.

But that possibility had remained as such. The results spoke for themselves.

Masato had been sucked into a video game, and just as he was certain he was about to embark on a wonderful tale of heroism in this new world…he found his mother with him.

And his mother was so ridiculously powerful she made the ostensible hero look absolutely worthless.

What's more, the win condition for the game he'd been pulled into required he get along with his mother—a goal clearly set by some absolute sadist.

As nightmarish as that mission sounded, Masato had accepted it.

And yet.

I can't keep moaning and sulking. I've just got to do what I can.

Accept his present situation and take steps to improve it. Think about what those steps might be. Masato was slowly getting better at that approach.

Did that qualify as growth? He allowed himself a pat on the back.

"Well, now that I'm feeling better, our current target…is this!"

Masato pulled a flyer out of his pocket. He unfolded it, and ran his eyes across the page again.

In big letters across the top it read:

NEW TOWER DUNGEON GRAND OPENING!

It sure read like a realty listing—like, it had clearly been intentionally designed to evoke that feel. Was management just goofing around? *They really ought to put more effort into a consistent tone here*, Masato thought...but he elected not to voice this complaint aloud.

Below the header, it continued:

THOSE WHO CLEAR THE DUNGEON WILL HAVE A SINGLE WISH GRANTED!

He read this again, just to be sure. It even had a footnote that said: *REALLY!

This was an unprecedented reward.

Any wish at all?

Masato thought long and hard about this. What should he ask for?

The first thing that came to mind was the abolishment of the sadistic requirement that his mother accompany him, but they'd also included a footnote that read: *DOES NOT INCLUDE EXCEPTIONS TO PARENT-RELATED DESIGN, SUCH AS THE PARENT-CHILD PAIRING REQUIREMENT. Plus: *ALSO EXCLUDES IMMEDIATELY BEATING THE GAME.

Below *that*, it read, *NO WISHING FOR MORE WISHES and *VAGUE EXPRESSIONS SUCH AS "PEAK CONDITION" WILL NOT BE ACCEPTED. By this point, the lettering was getting quite small and hard to read. There was a reason they called it "the fine print," but this was getting a little ridiculous. How overprepared could they be?

It seemed like the wishes they granted were limited to specific elements of game progression.

Hmm... In that case, I guess finding some way to make myself stronger...

If he could just be stronger than his mother, then he could have a lot of fun being the OP protagonist. That sounded good. Like, perfect.

So how exactly should he phrase the request? Learn the strongest skill? No, no, max stats? Hmm... This was tricky...

Just then.

"Hey, Masatooo! What are you doing? Don't just stand there, come on!"

"Huh? ...O-oh, right behind you!"

He'd been thinking so hard he'd stopped in his tracks. Wise was way ahead of him, and he hurried to catch up with her and the other party members.

Wise took one look at the flyer in his hand, and a smile spread over her lips so clearly malicious he reflexively wanted to slap her.

"Y'know, I do hate to burst the bubble of your inflated expectations..." She grinned devilishly.

"Shut up, Wise. I already know what you're going to say, so just don't."

"Okay, okay, I'll spare you this time. Medhi and Porta will say it for me."

"Huh? I will?"

"Eep?! Me too?!"

"Someone's gotta say it, right? And it's gotta be before he comes face-to-face with the harsh reality and gets roasted in the process. If we tell him now, he'll come away relatively unscathed. Am I wrong?"

"Well... I do think you've got a point there..."

"Eep... Maybe we should do something... Masato's going to be so disappointed otherwise..."

"Exactly! We're just being kind. So..."

Medhi and Porta had not been expecting to get dragged into this, but Wise wasn't about to let that stop her. She had them thinking now.

And with that, the two of them turned on Masato.

"Um, Masato. I do hate to be rude, but if you don't mind..."

"I would also like to say what I think!"

"Yeah... Yeah. We're all friends here. No need to hold back. Both of you can say your piece."

"Then..."

Medhi and Porta looked at each other. They decided Medhi should start.

"That flyer you're so interested in was obtained in a highly suspicious manner, wasn't it?"

"Yeah, fair enough. They made it look like a flyer being passed out everywhere, yet it was delivered directly to my room at the inn. No signs of any left outside anyone else's door."

"I took a look at it myself, and the fine print really bothered me!

...They make it sound like there's a special prize for anyone attending, but..."

"Right. The only job that can actually claim that special prize is the Normal Hero's Mother. And my mom is the only person with that job. This flyer description is clearly targeting us specifically."

"So..."

"That means...!"

"I know! Don't spell it out."

He held up a hand to stop them and closed his eyes.

This was, unmistakably, beyond a shadow of a doubt, bait designed to hook them.

He could easily imagine the implacable features of the Mysterious Nun who was attempting to lure them in.

This was obviously her scheme. Nothing else made sense.

Yeah, I know! I know...

Masato wasn't an idiot. He'd known the second he'd seen the flyer. However... Even so... He just...

"But...I want to get stronger than Mom and actually enjoy my adventures! That's all I want! I want that more than anything! I'm desperate here!"

Masato was definitely getting a little emotional. A gush of hot tears welled up in his eyes.

"Ew, gross." "Th-that's a bit..." "Passionate...?"

Masato was about to have an even bigger outburst, but before he could...

"Ma-kun, now, now, don't cry."

Mamako reached out her hand and cradled his head, pulling his tearstained face into the warmth of her bosom. The sweet, calming mother's scent... Wait!

"Hey, Mom! What's the big idea?!"

"Don't worry. Mommy's always on your side. You just do what you want to do, okay? So don't cry. Mommy is here for you." *Squeeze!*

"R-right, okay! Glad to hear it! Now lemme go! Medhi and Porta are laughing at me! And Wise has a nasty little smirk on her face!"

"How dare you! Never call a girl's face 'nasty'!" *Raaaage!*

Wise seemed pretty much ready to bite him, and she was definitely not cute when she was angry.

But she was good at getting him back.

"You piss me off! I don't care anymore! I really wasn't going to go there, but if you're gonna act like that, I'll spell it out for you."

"S-spell what out?"

"I'm a Sage, remember? The ultimate Sage? I've got a special power that lets me see a tiny glimpse of the future. Like, for real."

"Oh?" Medhi said. "Wise, you've never mentioned this before?!"

"That's amazing!" Porta gasped. "I really respect you, Wise!"

"Yo, you two, remember, she's probably talking out of her—"

"And I already know what the future holds in store for you. First, we're gonna hit up this dungeon, right? And Mamako's gonna clear the whole thing for us like always. And we're gonna get to the part where our wish is granted, and there…"

"What?"

"What's gonna happen?"

"Just as Masato is about to make his wish, Mamako will be all, 'Oh my, I forgot to buy eggs for breakfast tomorrow. I wish I had some eggs.' Or something like that."

And then a basket of eggs would drop into Masato's hands. Hooray. That seemed…

Entirely plausible. Mamako had been known to do that.

"Um, Wise…? You're really scaring me now… Please say that isn't true."

"Don't worry, Ma-kun. Mommy will make sure to wish for freshly laid eggs. Oh, right, I would also make sure to ask for enough eggs for everybody!"

"Ugggghhh!! Moooom, stop making it woooorse!! Listen, do NOT say anything like that! Make no wishes! Ever!"

"Riiight, everyone! Let's go off and witness the moment when my prediction becomes reality!"

"A quest to get delicious eggs!"

"It isn't!! Porta, that's not the goal here!! This is a quest to get my wish granted, not an egg run!!"

The girls chattered as Masato shrieked. Always a lively party.

Mamako maintained a firm grip on Masato's head as they set off once more…unaware that they were heading toward an event that would decide their very fates. Kinda.

But of course, they had no way of knowing that! They were just heading for a tower.

The village was called Thermo.

It was a coastal town built along a crescent-shaped bay. The blue of the ocean and the orange roofs made for a colorful view, and the white sails of the ships billowing in the salty sea breeze as they sailed in and out of the harbor were as beautiful as a painting.

But it was the tower on an island in the bay that drew the eye.

At the end of a single long bridge running from the coast was a tower so tall it looked more like a pillar holding the sky up. This was the tower dungeon the flyer had advertised.

Even from a distance they'd known the tower was very tall, but seen from the Thermo entrance, it was overwhelming. The girls all stared up at it, making impressed noises.

"Wow. It's like the dungeon's right here in town. Easy access! …But still, that's *really* tall."

"Yes… I wonder how many floors there are…"

"I can't even see the top! That's *very* tall!"

"Getting up there will be quite tough… I do hope there's an elevator."

If it were that easy to get to the top, the place would've been cleared by now, Masato thought.

But he had bigger fish to fry right now.

"What should I do? What should I do?! …If I don't find a way of restraining her worst impulses, I really will end up with a basket of eggs… At the very least, I've gotta find a way to keep my wish from turning into breakfast… But how? What can I do…?"

Masato was really worried about this now. This *was* Mamako, after all. She was constantly doing the unpredictable—glowing, floating, what have you—and how could you possibly restrain what you couldn't predict?

Just then—

"Oh! You must be adventurers! How lovely! Would you be so kind as to help search for my child?"

"...Uh?"

—the second he stepped into the town, someone started talking to him.

Masato abandoned his line of thought and looked up to find a middle-aged woman. She was standing at the head of a group of other middle-aged women.

Masato got the overwhelming impression:

Are they all...mothers?

He wasn't sure what gave him that idea. It was just a general motherly vibe.

But he wasn't given a chance to ponder the source of that vibe. He was immediately surrounded by the crowd of mothers.

"Please! Listen to my story! It's just awful!"

"Same here! I'm so worried! I haven't eaten a thing!"

"She often leaves suddenly without saying a word, but this time is different!"

"He said he was going to the tower and he never came back! How can I not worry?"

"Oh, he did? Mine too!"

"Same here! Do you know anything? Anything at all? Please tell me if you do!"

"Oh, can I ask, too? We'll share anything we have!"

"Er... Um... Uh... Wh-what...?"

One second the crowd was trying to get his attention, and then a moment later, they were all chattering away to one another. What was even going on? He was so lost. Clearly something bad was happening, but beyond that...

The rest of his party joined him, attracted by the commotion, but they appeared equally confused.

"Oh my! Whatever is going on here?"

"Seems like they're all getting worked up...but I'm not entirely sure just what the problem is..."

"I can't even hear myself think! The heck's all this yapping about?"

"Uh, uh, uh, M-Masato! What's happening?!"

"Sorry. I've got no clue. Our only choice...is to get her to explain."
Masato looked across the crowd to the edge of the road.

There stood a coffin. Only one person they knew always showed up unexpectedly dead. "Oh, she's here!" "Wow, she totally is." "She is!" "Huh? Who is that?" This was Medhi's first time encountering this situation, but everyone else knew exactly who it was.

As desperate as the pack of mothers had been to talk to Masato, they had now entirely forgotten him, talking only among themselves. Too busy gossiping to get around to the point... Perhaps that was just part of being a mother.

Taking advantage of this, Masato's party slipped away from the crowd, picked up the coffin, and moved into a back road. Out of consideration for the person inside, nobody grumbled about how heavy it was.

"Okay! Wise, would you be so kind?"

"Wise has great revival spells!"

"You're up."

"Yeah, yeah, I'll take care of it, hold your horses."

Their Sage could easily handle revival magic. Wise produced her tome and got ready to cast...

But then Medhi stopped her.

"Um, Wise, hold on. Would you mind leaving this to me? I am the party's healer, after all."

"Oh... Right, right. I guess this is your job. Go ahead!"

"Thank you. Let's see now... *Spara la magia per mirare... Rianimato!*"

The light of Rianimato poured from Medhi's staff onto the coffin below. Cura and Rianimato were a Healer's stock in trade, a chance for a Cleric like Medhi to shine.

Meanwhile...

"Hmm... One less chance for Wise to actually finish casting a spell, huh?"

"Ahhh!! Medhi just stole one of my few chances to do anything!!"

The Sage reeled from this shocking truth. The Healer's smile betrayed just a hint of a gloat. That aside...

The spell complete, everyone's favorite nun sat up in the coffin. Maintaining her usual placid beauty, she looked around and bowed her head.

"I see everyone's here. Nice to meet you again. I am Shiraaase. I must infooorm you that coming up with new names and outfits every time has proven to be quite a pain, so we're just going to stick with this one."

"Thanks for the infooormation."

"Do whatever you like, see if we care."

"Hee-hee. You are such a strange person, Ms. Shiraaase."

"Ms. Shiraaase is always the same no matter where we find her!"

"It's been quite a while since we last met, Ms. Shiraaase... Now, if I may..."

"Why was I dead, you ask? Very well. I shall satisfy your morbid curiosity, Medhi, and infooorm you of the particulars."

"Huh? No, you don't need to explain that."

"I don't...?"

Faced with this flat rejection, Shiraaase's eyes opened 30 percent wider than usual, and she gave Medhi a long look. A long, loooong look. Horrible emotions appeared to be writhing somewhere beneath the surface. This could be real bad. "Er, um, okay! I'd love to hear about it!"

"That's what I thought."

It would never do to interfere with Shiraaase's infooormative briefings. Medhi had learned a valuable lesson.

"As to my death this time," Shiraaase infooormed them, "this specific cause was once again a fatal bug. A mere touch of the hedge at the side of the road and it was all over."

"Another deadly bug? There are way too many of those. What's the testing team doing?"

"As you say, Masato. Though I am technically part of operations, I, too, fill my spare minutes with testing and end up dying on a daily basis...but this time that bug may have saved me."

"Huh? How can a fatal bug save you? What's that even mean?"

"In truth, like the rest of you, I was swarmed by all the mother NPCs in town, begging me for assistance. But I am an admin. I cannot progress events designed for players. Which means..."

"You avoided triggering the event by dying. I see! That could be seen as salvation. Can you go ahead and infooorm us about the particulars of this event?"

"Yes, well… Hmm…"

Masato had expected Shiraaase to launch right into it, but instead she appeared to be lost in thought.

Then she stood up.

"Before I infooorm you about that, I must verify a few things. I do apologize for the trouble, but would you mind accompanying me to explore the tower? We need only check out the easier lower levels, so if you could be so kind…"

"Er… Uh, sure, that's no problem."

"Thank you very much. Let us make haste. This way!"

Shiraaase led Masato's party quickly in the direction of the tower.

It was rare to see any crack in her iron wall of placidity, but she definitely seemed mildly unsettled today.

The tower was within the town limits, on an island in the bay at the end of a long bridge from the shore.

The tower was just too big. It was incredibly tall and extremely wide. Up close, not only did it fill one's vision, it appeared to simply be an immense wall that went on forever.

There was a giant door at the base of this massive tower.

"This appears to be the way in, but the door is shut tight. How do we…? Hm? What the…?"

As Masato stepped toward the door, a small magic circle appeared at his feet. Similar circles appeared at the feet of his companions…

…and a moment later, the door slowly opened.

"Hmm, that much is by design."

"Design…? Shiraaase, was that…?"

"I shall explain the details later. For now, let's step inside. I request your assistance with an urgent evaluation of the current state of affairs."

"Uh, sure… Got it."

Shiraaase moved forward, her manner almost flustered, and they followed her inside the tower.

The first floor. Inside, it was a dimly lit stone dungeon. Corridors wide enough for them to walk in a pack, stretching away into the distance.

"The name of this dungeon is the Solo-Killer Tower."

"Solo...Killer..."

"What a terrifying name!"

"Don't worry, Mamako. 'Solo killer' just means the tower is impossible to complete alone. The name itself infooorms players they will not be able to complete the dungeon in single-player. It is no cause for concern."

"A dungeon you can't solo, huh? That would definitely lead to a lot of dying. But how many floors is it?"

"Oh, one hundred."

"That many? That seems like a lot... Although, from the view outside, it seems unnaturally low..."

"Right you are, Medhi. During the planning stages, it was intended to be ten thousand floors, but since asking real flesh-and-blood humans doing a full dive to climb that many stories seemed a bit much, the number was drastically reduced."

"T-ten thousand?! Even if this was a normal game, I don't think I could ever make it through that many floors..."

"*Tch, tch,* kids these days, no attention span. I myself have climbed ten thousand floors before, you know. All the way up the Spectral Tower. Not to go on a tangent."

On they went.

This was definitely a dungeon. And that meant... "Oh my, monsters! *Hyah!*" Mamako's two-hit multi-target attacks easily dispatched all manner of terrifying foes while the rest of the party just watched impassively, like they had long since achieved enlightenment.

This went on for a while until they reached a wide-open space.

At first glance, it appeared to be a perfectly ordinary room...but there were a few strange elements to it. The floor was paved with square tiles that had different symbols carved into them: medicine bottles, bags, magic tomes, and whirlwinds.

"Um, Shiraaase...? Those things on the floor... Uh... Are they...?"

"You noticed? I imagine they are precisely what you're thinking. This dungeon interior has a number of effects designed to activate if you set foot on the wrong portion of the floor. This was the intended design... So, Masato, why don't you try stepping on that medicine bottle icon?"

"All right. Here goes... Hup!"

Masato stepped on the stone with the medicine bottle. A light filled with life force poured out, wrapping around his body.

Masato's HP was restored!

"Oh, that's what I thought. Right, I've played a game like this."

"I imagine you have. That's it in a nutshell. The medicine icon is recovery. As for the bag... Well, let's have Porta try that out."

"Okay! I'll step right on it!"

Porta dashed over where Shiraaase pointed, jumped as high as she could, and stomped on the floor panel. A key appeared in front of her.

Porta obtained Exit Key!

"Wow! An item appeared! That's amazing!"

"I'll explain how to use that special item later. Next..."

"Yeah, yeah, my turn now! I just step on the squares marked with the magic tome and that'll power up my magic, right? Those are totally for me! Outta my way!!"

Without waiting for an answer, Wise stomped on several tome marks in a row.

A sinister mist poured out. "H-huh?" The mist wrapped itself around Wise.

Wise's magic was sealed!

"...What...the...?" *Shock!*

"Wise has just stepped on a magic seal trap disguised as a magic-up square. Additionally, the trap effects are different from the status effects in battle, so you can't heal them with items or magic. And they stack based on the number of squares you activate."

"They...whaaaat?! Whyyyyyyyyyyyyyyyyyyyyy?!"

"Yikes... You really did it this time..."

"Ohh... If items can't fix this, there's nothing I can do..." Porta wailed.

"Oh dear. If it stacks for each time you activated it... Wise stepped on so many squares... Does that mean she'll never be able to use magic again...?"

"M-M-M-Mamakooooooo?! You're really scaring meeeeee!!"

Wise was finished. "No, wait!" They no longer had anything to say that could help her now. "Come on, say something! Hey!" A look of gloom settled over the party's faces, and they avoided meeting Wise's gaze as she started ugly crying. "Look! Look at me! I'm right here!" Their former friend, Wise, was no more...

But then...

"Wise, don't worry!" Medhi said cheerily. She gave her best angelic smile and put her arms around Wise.

"Oh... Medhi... My one true friend..." Wise beamed as if she'd just been pulled back from the brink of death. Friendship between girls was truly a thing of beauty.

"Wise, you can just leave the rest to me. Thank you for everything you've done." *Smirk!*

"Whaaaaaaat?! Are you giving me a send-off?!"

"With Wise gone, I'm the party's only Mage...and having secured that key position, I'll get plenty of chances to shine... All right!"

"How could you?! Medhi!! Medhiiii!! Has the dark power within you finally corrupted your last shred of decency?! But seriously, what am I gonna do...?"

"Oh, Wise, Wise, good news! Somewhere in the dungeon is a floor that will undo all the traps. Additionally, the trap effects are only active within this dungeon, so all you have to do is leave the dungeon once and the effect will be canceled."

"Oh, really? Geez, Shiraaase! Tell me that sooner."

"...*Tch.*"

"Medhiiii! How dare someone as beautiful as you go around clicking your tongue like that!!"

Wise came off her emotional roller coaster in a rage and threw herself at the evil beauty Medhi! Looks like a catfight's about to break out! But the rest of the party simply said things like, "Look how close they've grown!" "Let's call it that, sure." "Okay!" In other words, they decided they were better off staying out of this one.

There was one more type of special icon: a stone slab with a whirl-wind symbol.

"Now then, let me introduce the final effect. I particularly wanted Medhi to test this one for us, but she seems otherwise occupied... Mamako, can I ask your help?"

"Me? Certainly. I don't mind at all."

"Uh, Mom, wait... At least make her say what it is first..."

"Don't worry. The whirlwind mark is incredibly beneficial to dungeon progression. Calm yourself and observe. This will likely serve as a reward for you, Masato. Heh-heh-heh."

"A reward for me? ...Does that mean...?"

Shiraaase's meaningful smirk just made him even more suspicious.

"Then I'll hop right on! Here I go!"

But before he could stop her, Mamako jumped right onto the square.

"...Huh? Nothing's happening?"

"No, the effect is already activated. Look above Mamako's head."

"Above her? ...Oh!"

When he looked up, there was a hole yawning in the ceiling, and they could see through to the floor above.

An instant later, a powerful wind swirled up around Mamako's feet.

"O-oh? Eeeek!"

The gust of wind caused Mamako's dress to balloon upward and flip inside out.

Masato watched as his mother's underwear flashed right before his very eyes!

Mom was wearing panties and stockings! Her waist: slim! Her legs: slim! Even the panties seen through the stockings: rather slim!

Panties and stockings exposed, Mamako was wafted up to the floor above.

Masato sank to the ground in a heap, burying his face in his knees.

"I'm begging you...don't do stuff like that. That isn't a reward. It's retribution. I'm already suffering... I've already suffered so much..."

How was he supposed to live with these feelings? Any boy would feel the same after getting an eyeful of his mother's panty-and-stocking-clad nether regions. Probably.

Shiraaase put a hand on his shoulder. "Don't worry," she whispered. "Someday you'll understand…just how great panties and stockings are."

If Masato were just a little more mature, would he develop a taste for these things and look upon them with feelings of bliss?

HELL no. Not as long as they were on his mom.

The whirlwind mark effect allowed you to jump up to the floor above. It was helpful in that it allowed you to avoid a lengthy search for the stairs.

Masato had received a critical blow to his psyche, but even he had to admit this was useful. His party all moved to the floor above and continued to progress using either stairs or the tiles as they found them.

They were currently on the ninth floor.

"Guys, seriously. If you find a jump tile, just let me know. I'll hop on it first. I don't wanna see that kind of spectacle ever again."

"You don't ever want to see me again? Mommy is so sad!" *Sniffle!*

"Perhaps tomorrow you should go without panties or stockings. That would delight Masato, I'm sure."

"Absolutely not!! Mom, I don't need to see your bare legs, either! I don't need to see any of that!"

"Oh, Wise, here's another tile for you! Go ahead."

"Why do you keep trying to make me step on the traps? Geez… Medhi, you and I need to have a long talk one of these days…"

The party moved forward, chattering away. Of course, this was a dungeon, and monsters did show up, but the ones on the lower floors were all small fries, and with Mamako by their side…

"*Hyah!*"

…not much else needed to be said.

Then Porta, who had the sharpest eyes, spotted something.

"…Oh! Stairs!"

"Whoa, good job, Porta! Let's go!"

They went up the stairs to the tenth floor.

It was a fairly large room—no corridors, just a giant closed door at the back.

"Well, this seems obvious enough... Shiraaase, you're up."

"Allow me to explain. Every tenth floor of this dungeon is an open space where the stratum boss is located. A pretty typical pattern, really."

"Okay, boss fight time! Finally, I get to do something! Since we found a trap removal tile just now, I can use magic again! My chain cast will—!"

"But your magic was sealed," Medhi whispered.

"Medhiiiiiiii!! Don't you dare even joke about thaaaat!!"

"Eek! Wise, you're so scary!"

Wise was at her throat again. Medhi sure did have an evil grin for someone so beautiful. The girls appeared poised to have another fight, but...

...Masato just ignored it, asking Shiraaase more questions.

"So where exactly is this stratum boss?"

"We have the required number of people present, so any minute now... Oh, the count's begun. It will show up soon. Be on your guard."

Just like they had at the entrance, a set of magic circles appeared at the party's feet.

A moment later, the big door opened with an ominous creak. "Right, here it comes!" Masato drew his sword. Mamako pulled her two swords while Porta retreated to safety. "Wise!" "On it!" The two girls quit grappling and got ready for combat.

A sinister aura lurked behind the giant door, hinting at the spawn of something massive.

"*Mroooww!*"

With a shrill cry, a cat-shaped monster appeared!

But the size of it was exactly the same as an ordinary cat. Tiny. "Oh, a kitty!" "A cat?!" "It's so cute." "I love kitty cats!" It proved quite popular with the girls.

"Um... Shiraaase...? Is that the boss?"

"It is the first boss. They're mostly like this. Easily finished by a single blow from the hero."

"Uh, sure, okay..."

Masato strolled over to the kitten boss, and it didn't seem like he really needed to bother taking a swing at it, so he just tapped it lightly with the flat of his blade. *"Meow?! ...Mmrrr..."*

OVERKILL!

Masato's overwhelming power mercilessly defeated his foe!

All the girls were staring at him, totally silent. Baleful.

"Ugh... No, no! ...It was a monster! It's not like I was being mean to it or anything..."

"It can be a challenge dealing with cute monsters in games. The creators may have thought it was a good idea, but for the players who must defeat it... Well, perhaps that's not for me to say... Hmm..."

"Ms. Shiraaase? What's the matter?"

"So far, everything is as it should be... The tower itself appears unaltered..."

Shiraaase appeared to be reaching some conclusion known only to her. Then...

"Oh? I'm surprised to find anyone actually climbing the tower. I thought I'd placed every adventurer in town under my control. There were still some left?"

Someone's mumbling carried past the large open door up ahead. The person was coming down the stairs beyond the door.

It was a girl. She wore light armor, a black coat hanging off her shoulders, and a thin sword at her hip. Her job was most likely Fencer.

She seemed roughly the same age as Masato. Definitely pretty cute, but she had a wild stallion ponytail that made her look quite aggressive.

Then... "Ah...?!" She slipped on the stairs—"Oof!"—fell flat on her ass, and then kept going, bouncing down one stair after another. This looked quite painful.

"Whoa... Are you okay there?"

"I-it's none of your concern! I did not fall!"

No, you totally slipped and fell.

Like nothing had happened—or like she wanted nothing to have happened—the girl quickly scrambled to her feet and adjusted her gear.

And then she shot the party a look of naked hostility.

"Uh... So... Who are you?"

"Who am I? Doesn't matter. I am one of the Four Heavenly Kings of the Libere Rebellion. We reject the concept of mothers. I am Anti-Mom Amante. Not that there's any rule saying you have to give your name to a total stranger. Is there?"

"Uh, no, I guess not..."

She gave her name, though. He'd definitely heard a name. Maybe she was a total moron.

The Four Heavenly Kings of the Libere Rebellion? Reject the concept of mothers? Anti-Mom Amante?

Amante had certainly said a lot of words, but none of them made any sense to him.

"Uh... So... Maybe you could maybe explain all that in, like...detail?"

"You think I'd bother giving you a detailed explanation? The Libere Rebellion is an organization that fights against parents everywhere, so why would I bother explaining that, too...? Mm?"

Just as she had begun to blab a detailed explanation for Masato's query, she suddenly shut her mouth.

She gave Mamako a long look and then gasped.

"Wha...? No way, a-are you...?"

"Hm? Oh, how lovely to meet you! I'm Mamako Oosuki, Ma-kun's mother! Hee-hee."

"You don't need to introduce yourself, let alone tell her you're my mom."

They also had someone who insisted on always politely introducing herself to everyone they met, but moving right along.

"You can't be... Really? The real Mamako Oosuki?! ...Gah!"

For some reason, Amante suddenly turned on her heel and ran.

"Uh, hey! What the heck?!"

"I'm not going to stop and explain why we're on guard against Mamako Oosuki, but I am going to hightail it outta here! ...Mamako Oosuki's party has only six people. And no chance of increasing their numbers. You have no way of climbing all the way up to us, so there's no chance of you following me... I'm better off retreating here and planning countermeasures!"

Talking to herself in a clearly audible voice, Amante ran off up the stairs...

...and a moment later, her foot slipped, and she bashed her shin hard. "Unhhh!" Masato got that it hurt, but maybe girls shouldn't put out quite such a throaty grunt?

Amante proceeded to come tumbling down the stairs to the ground, where she lay writhing in agony, glaring up at Mamako like it was her fault.

"Arrrgh! I'll make you regret subjecting me to this indignity! You will pay!"

Guarding her throbbing shin, Amante scrambled back up the stairs on all fours.

Mamako's mouth was hanging open, the baseless charge against her coming as a complete surprise. Masato didn't blame her. He, Wise, Medhi, and Porta were all equally stunned. The whole thing had seemed entirely pointless.

"Um... H-hey, Ma-kun? Who was that just now?"

"That's what I wanna know! So...Shiraaase? What exactly was that pitiable creature I was reluctant to even look at for fear of cringing? I could really use an explanation here."

He passed the question on from Mamako.

Shiraaase, who had been watching the entire thing without batting an eye, nodded.

"Very well. I have a grasp of the current situation now, so let us retreat outside for a briefing. Porta, try using the key you obtained earlier."

"Oh, okay! I can do that!"

Porta pulled the Exit Key out of her shoulder bag and held it aloft. A door appeared in front of her. She used the key to open it and..."Wow! It's the outside!"...through the door they could see the landscape in front of the tower entrance.

"Let us go through. This way!" Shiraaase beckoned them, and they followed her out of the tower.

Outside, it was already evening. Bathed in the light of the setting sun, the coastal town had turned a lovely shade of red. It was a beautiful sunset, but there was something sad about it, a fragile air.

They left the island, heading back to town. As they crossed the long bridge, Shiraaase, in the lead, suddenly paused.

"There's a nice breeze blowing, so why don't we talk here?"

She leaned against the railing. The sea breeze brushed against her cheeks, tinged with a hint of sorrow. If she were anyone else, she would have seemed quite lovely.

But Masato was less focused on her beauty than the rare glimpse of genuine emotion.

"Masato. This is not the time to be gazing adoringly at the mother of a five-year-old girl."

"I was doing no such thing!! Argh! I guess Shiraaase will always be Shiraaase."

"Indeed I will. I am Shiraaase! The Mysterious Nun and a lowly admin for this game world… Or one who demands hard labor, both physical and mental, and keeps you all moving forward… That is who I am."

She spoke softly, almost as if trying to convince herself. Then she turned to face them.

"First," she began, "I must honestly infooorm you that I had no prior knowledge of the situation occurring in town."

"…Huh?"

This reveal came as a bit of a shock.

"Um…but aren't you an admin, Shiraaase? You've always seemed to have a firm grasp on everything that was going on."

"Indeed. It is just as you say, Mamako. I have been your guide and previously led you into situations fully aware of the situation at hand and with a solid projection as to how it might play out."

"That makes it sound like we've just been dancing in the palm of your hand! That really pisses me off, you know. So…how come you don't know this time? Oh, wait, are you just saying this to trick us again? I get it. That's totally something you'd do."

"I'm afraid this time I genuinely don't know. Cross my heart."

Wise glared even harder, but Shiraaase was unperturbed.

"The town of Thermo is supposed to be just what the flyer says: a base of operations for people clearing the tower dungeon. But that isn't set up for just five of you; this is a trial for cooperative combat functions, and the goal would be to clear the tower while working with other test players and NPCs."

"Cooperative combat with other... Oh, I see. The magic circles out front are counting the number of people there, and if you don't hit the required number, the doors won't open, the stratum boss won't spawn, and you can't proceed... Is that how it works?"

"Well done, Medhi. I see you have the intelligence to back up your strict education. Exactly right. To conquer this tower, you must establish a guild and gather a certain number of participants."

"I see... And these cooperative combat functions are designed with an eye toward manipulating player consciousness?"

"Well done again, Medhi. Your own internal darkness makes you extra sensitive to the sinister. You are absolutely correct. By fighting together, peer pressure will convince you that you should be able to do what your allies are doing, and it will increase the desire to invest time and actively participate."

"I see. You sell it as cooperative, but that's the real goal. Heh-heh."

"It's the core grift of all online games. Heh-heh."

"Um, can the two of you knock that off, please?"

If they said any more, men in black were going to show up and take them away.

Then Porta's hand shot up. "Um, can I ask a question?"

"Yes, Porta. Go ahead."

"By 'guild,' do you mean something different from the place that gives us quests?"

"An excellent question. Yes, I do mean something different. The guild I just mentioned refers to a group of friends forming a team. It's a common term in video games."

"Oof... That's sort of confusing..."

"An excellent point. As you're all well aware, you are currently participating in the game's beta version. I believe we will have a more appropriate name for things once service officially begins, so please overlook the present awkwardness. This is a request from management."

Oh well. "That's a beta for you." "Yep." "Beta... Now that you mention it, Mommy was always more of a VHS person." "Huh? What's a VHS?" Let's just ignore the ramblings of the only one here old enough to remember the video format wars. Everyone agreed to pretend not to notice the term confusion.

Shiraaase suddenly looked downcast and wearily rubbed her temples.

"But everything is as it should be. This town was set up to support multiple guilds competing with one another to clear the tower first... However, it seems events have taken a rather different turn."

"Starting with the commotion at the town entrance, right? A whole crowd of mothers complaining that their children haven't come home..."

"Seems safe to assume they've all run away. Rebelling against their parents, striking out on their own..."

"And joining the Libere Rebellion, huh?"

"That girl was very insistent on explaining how they reject the very idea of parents."

"That was one of the Four Heavenly Kings of the Libere Rebellion, the Anti...Anti-Mom Amante!"

"Personally, I had no idea such a group even existed. This game is designed to deepen the bonds between parent and child, so for a group to spring up encouraging discord between them... I think we have to assume they're essentially a league of evil."

"And they've gone up the tower and are trying to make their evil wish come true. What that wish could be is a mystery, but...either way, something clearly needs to be done. By us."

Yep. This was where Masato's party came in.

As the party hero, Masato should say something noble. Totally. This was his moment to shine.

Masato took a deep breath, preparing to speak...

"Then, to shatter their evil ambitions, we must—!"

"Let's all help get these runaway children back home!" Mamako piped up, totally drowning him out. Oh, Mamako.

Masato was annoyed that she'd interrupted him again, but he wasn't a kid. He was capable of being generous and forgiving. He kept his voice calm.

"Um, Mom...? Can we talk?"

"O-oh? You seem even angrier than usual..."

"It's not that I'm angry… Anyway—what am I talking about? That's not the point here. This is where our heroic party takes a stand to defeat evil."

"Mm… That's true, but Mommy is much more worried about getting these children safely home than the fate of the world."

Most moms would be. Major world problems just didn't matter the way their children's problems did. Their children were everything to them. Particularly to Mamako.

"So Mommy thinks our main goal here should be to bring back all the children who ran away. Don't you agree?"

"Well…" As Masato considered this, the others joined in.

"I totally agree," Wise said. "If we get the kids back, that reduces the enemy's numbers. Then they won't be able to clear the tower, and their evil ambitions will be thwarted. It all works out!"

"Th-that's true, yeah…"

"So the question is, how do we get them back? If the children are under enemy control, and they're all in the tower slowly working their way up it…then we'll have to climb the tower after them," added Medhi.

"O-oh, right. Then…"

"And if we've got to climb the tower, we'll have to form a guild!"

"Yeah, I thought the same thing. So…"

"Yes, exactly. Let's make a guild!"

"Yeah, okay. That's what I was about to… Oh, but our number of members is a big issue—"

"Well done, Mamako. You've gotten straight to the heart of it. Let's get ready to establish a guild. First, we need to secure a base…"

"R-right, I can do that! I'll go find us a good—!"

"Just as the flyer infooormed you, we have prepared a special prize for the Normal Hero's Mother, Mamako. This way. Power of the State! Forcible Transport!"

A technique powered not by magic but by admin rights.

No sooner had the words left Shiraaase's mouth than the party vanished from the bridge…

…and a moment later, they were on the outskirts of Thermo, standing on a plateau with a view of the ocean, the tower, and the town.

A ruined building stood beside them.

"Uh... Is this...an inn?"

It looked like it had been an inn once. You could just barely make out the word INN on the sign. It seemed to have been abandoned for a while. The door and windows were all broken, and the wind was sweeping right through the place, and there was even grass growing inside.

Shiraaase pointed at the inn and said, "We're presenting Mamako with this land and the building on it. Please use it to establish your guild."

"Oh my. Can I really?"

"Ack... One more thing taken care of... And it's so run-down..."

"This is just a start. Expand this base, increase your membership, and enjoy running your own guild... Well then, Mamako, now that you have a base, it should be possible to submit the application to found a guild. Please fill out the necessary fields on this form and submit it. Quickly!"

"Okay, got it!" *Quickly!*

"Hello? Anyone? I'm right here! I'm the hero! The party leader! Shouldn't I be the one filling out the...? Oh..."

The application screen in the air in front of Mamako had a field for listing the names of the designated representative and other members. "Ah!" Mamako entered her own name in the designated representative field. "Ahh!" She moved right along to the field for the guild name.

Guild Name: Mom's Guild

She was clearly putting no thought into this at all.

"And submitted!" *Click!*

"Aughhhhhhhhhhh?!"

Even a fearless battle-scarred adventurer would hesitate to identify himself as a member of that guild, but that was now their official name.

The birth of a mom guild by a mom and for moms, Mom's Guild.

And Masato was left watching his party get all excited without him.

"I feel like our adventure...would get on just fine without me," he muttered.

Mom's Guild Daily Report

Occupation: Mom (or should I say Guild Master?)
Name: Mamako Oosuki

Business Report:

Today, we established Mom's Guild. Many children have run away from home to a tower and gotten mixed up with a rough crowd there, so I think we need to gather some members quickly in order to get those kids back. I'm going to work hard with Ma-kun and the others!

Other Notes:

Well, I thought I'd write about the inn that's serving as our guild's base.
Mom's Guild Inn, Oosuki Ryokan (name not final). Six rooms for a maximum of fifteen guests. Parking for carriages available. All rooms have views and scenic baths.
The inn is located on a plateau with a lovely view of the town and ocean. I'd also like to provide some home cooking as a mother's personal touch. I eagerly await any and all guests and members who stay with us!

Member Comments:

We're only looking for members, not guests. Get it right.

By "rooms with views and scenic baths," you mean they don't have any windows or walls...

It certainly is true that the rooms provide an excellent view. The description is technically accurate.

I can't recommend Mama's food enough! Come and get some!

Chapter 2 At Mom's Guild, Business Is Booming!
...But We'd Be Better Off Without These
Guests!

Morning.

For Masato, it was the first morning in a long time that actually felt like a morning.

Oh, right... That's what mornings are like...

Bright light on his closed lids. Actual morning light. How refreshing!

For quite a while now, Masato had been resting in peace after the instant-death spell Wise always cast on him in the evening.

He'd gotten used to Alzare in a coffin, so all this light threw him for a loop, but this was a *real* morning. How he *should* be waking up. Masato opened his eyes, feeling amazing...

"Oh, you're up? Morning, Ma-kun!"

"Mm, morning... Wait... Mom?!"

...only to see Mamako's face was inches from his. If he'd lifted his head at all, there'd have been some forbidden contact. "Mmf!!" Masato desperately flattened himself against the bed.

"M-Mom! What are you doing?!"

"Breakfast is ready, so I came to wake you up! Everyone else is already awake, and you're the only sleepyhead still in bed."

"Right, right! I'm sorry! I'll get up, so please just get off of me! You're in my way!"

"In your way...? *Sniff*... You're making me cry."

"Don't cry! You seriously need a thicker skin than that! ...Arghhh! I'm sorry! I shouldn't have put it that way! I'm getting up now!"

Masato pushed Mamako out of the way and hopped down off the rather rustic bed.

The floor beneath his feet let out a creak...followed by a snap.

"Augh!! The floorboard broke?!"

"Oh my goodness! Ma-kun, are you okay?! Did you get hurt?!"

"Uh, no, I'm fine. You don't need to baby me like that. Geez..."

Mamako had seized her chance, and Masato was forced to push her back, pulling his foot out of the floor. Fortunately, he didn't get cut. Whew.

Masato had been sleeping in one of the rooms in Mom's Guild. Except for the bed, there was nothing in the room—it was maybe a bit too minimalist.

And there were no windows, doors, or even frames for those; there were a number of cracks in the floor with weeds growing out of them. It was clearly a ruin of a room.

"*Sigh*... Here I thought it was the most pleasant morning I've had in a while, but it sure stopped being pleasant fast. There's a limit to how run-down a place can be... Was your room intact?"

"Yes. Porta's Item Creation took care of the decor, and the floor didn't break or anything. I think you should definitely have slept with me, Ma-kun."

"No, absolutely not. I rejected that idea, so you can give it a rest... Still..."

"Yes. We have to do something. So, Ma-kun..."

"Yeah, breakfast first, right? Let's eat!"

He was starving. Nutrition first. Masato took an enthusiastic step forward and immediately broke another floorboard. "Oh my! Ma-kun, are you okay?" "Grr, so many traps..." He'd done it again. This was his reality.

Mom's Guild had only just begun.

Breakfast was in the inn's dining room.

They had prioritized repairing the room the girls had slept in and had not had time for this room yet, so it was still a wreck. The legs on the dining hall table had broken and rendered it unusable, so they had found a decent-sized board, propped it up on some rocks, and were using that as a makeshift table.

While the room might have been a mess, Mamako was here, so the food was flawless.

The hero, his mother, and a Sage on one side, the Cleric, the Traveling Merchant, and the nun on the opposite.

Rice, miso soup, eggs, natto, seasoned seaweed, and *furikake*, all eaten with chopsticks.

"A fantasy world…and a dining room that looks to predate even that. But whatever! Let's eat."

""""""Thanks for the food!"""""""

"Okay, eat up!"

Who cared about the setting? Neither the world nor the room was right for such a Japanese meal, but that was how they always started their mornings. This was an ironclad rule.

Swirling his chopsticks in an egg to pour over his rice, Masato spoke up first. He had something to talk about.

"Um…hey, everybody, listen up. I've got something I need to say."

"Oh, Ma-kun, what is it?"

"First, I'd like to add an item to the agenda pertaining to the name of our guild…"

"I'm afraid once a name is registered it can't be changed," Shiraaase said.

Shot down.

"Argh… Th-then let's think about the guild itself. We've made one, sure, but there's still a big problem. Remember what Amante said, especially the part about our numbers? …Hey, Wise, d'you remember?"

"Our numbers? …Umm… Oh, come to think of it, she did say we had no way of increasing them."

"Yes! Exactly! She put all the adventurers in town under her control. Leaving us with no way to increase our numbers."

"That certainly is a concern, but we have Mamako with us, so… won't that be enough?"

"No, um, Medhi… See, Mom being with us doesn't solve literally everything… Also, I'm here, too, y'know?"

"Mama makes the impossible possible! I feel like she does anyway!"

"Oof… Porta, clearly you have absolute faith in her, but…be that as it may, I've got a bad feeling about this… Also, I'm still here, y'know?"

The newly established Mom's Guild currently had five members. Shiraaase was an admin and unable to participate, so it was just the five of them.

If they couldn't increase their numbers somehow, getting to the top of the tower would be a challenge.

"It seems you will have to do something about the guild personnel. I will help in any way I can."

Shiraaase laid her chopsticks down. "Thanks for breakfast." "Oh, you're done already?" Shiraaase's plate was clean. That was quick.

"Today, I'll see what can be done from the operations side. I won't be back for a while, so please do take care. Oh, that's right. One piece of infooormation I mustn't forget to tell you."

"What?"

"I realized this hardly makes up for the trouble we're causing you, but I'd like to present you all with some gifts as a small token of our appreciation. I believe they've already been delivered to your item storage, so please take a look later on. So long!"

Shiraaase bowed politely and left the room.

Gifts?

"Gifts from Shiraaase... That just seems ominous..."

"Basically everything she gives us is for Mamako. Oh, but this time she did say 'all,' so maybe we get something, too?"

"I wonder what it could be! Should we check at once?"

"Okay! I'm so excited!"

"Hee-hee. Yes, I wonder what presents Ms. Shiraaase gave us."

Time for an item check. Everyone gently tapped the air in front of them, pulling up their status window. They clicked the ITEM selection and scrolled down their list of items.

And there! Astonishingly enough!

"Huh... It's actually not that bad."

"You're right. I really like it."

"I've never worn clothes like this before, so I'm really happy!"

Wise, Medhi, and Porta had all equipped the gifts from Shiraaase.

All three of them were wearing frilly dresses, the frills flouncing this way and that. There was even a frilly white thing on their heads.

"Hey, Master, if you want something, just spit it out! How 'bout that?" Wise called out cheekily.

"Wise, that language is hardly appropriate. This is how it should be done... Master, I await your instructions."

With the full power of her beauty on display, Medhi smiled and bowed.

"Um, um... Master! Please leave everything to me!" Porta piped up, as earnest as ever.

Three maids had appeared.

Masato stared at them, stunned, as if blinded by their maid smiles.

"Um..."

When he proved at a loss for words, a further maid attack activated!

Wise and Medhi both did a spin, their dresses billowing out, then put their hands together. "Kya-ha! ☆" "Heh-heh! ☆" A cheeky maid and a dark power maid buddy pose!

Then Porta did a spin, too. "Here goes... Whoa!" She almost lost her balance, but that just made it cuter! A cute and earnest little spin!

In the run-down entrance hall of the ruined inn, the sheer elegance of this attack left Masato reeling with bliss damage.

"Guh... Porta is one thing, but now I'm being charmed by Medhi and even Wise...!"

"What's that 'even' for? Just go ahead and drool over us. You're totally capable of being a creep like that!"

"That's right, Masato. Go right ahead and obsessively fawn over us like one of *those* boys who likes maids a little too much."

"If you weren't actively requesting it, I could happily fawn and drool all day!"

"Um, Masato! Do I look weird in this?"

"Nope, nope, not weird at all! You looks great!"

The tongue was made to spread evil. Even as he fawned over Porta, he forced himself to choke down a follow-up about how good Wise and Medhi looked.

Masato admired the three maid costumes Shiraaase had provided one more time and had to admit it.

"Hmm, well done... I honestly didn't expect much from Shiraaase's gifts, but she was really spot-on this time."

"Yeah. I might actually respect her a little now. This is really nice! It's the perfect size, too."

"Although in your case, Wise, the perfect size means perfectly flat..."

"Hey, Medhi, let's take this outside." *Twitch, twitch.*

"So what did you get, Masato?" Porta asked.

"Oh, me? I, uh...got the same thing."

Masato awkwardly held out a matching maid outfit. "Wow, congrats." "Congratulations." "Can't say I'm thankful." "We all match!"

"Y-yeah, I guess we do..." He was pretty sure there was a mistake here, but...it was his size and everything. Not that he'd tried it on. He'd just held it up to his shoulders a moment.

Anyway, all four of them now had maid costumes...

"Um, I just had a thought," Wise muttered. "If we all got the same thing, then..."

Just a moment later:

"Sorry to keep you all waiting! With the taps in the kitchen not working, washing up took *such* a long time... Oh? Oh my! So many adorable maids!"

There was Mamako. She came walking into the entrance hall, admiring the girls' outfits.

She was wearing her usual dress and apron.

"Huh? You're dressed all normal."

"Yeah... You aren't wearing a maid costume..."

"Did you get something different, Mamako?"

"Nah, Mom got the same thing. I just told her not to put it on. Everything Shiraaase gives out is a threat to my sanity, from the sailor uniform to the school swimsuit. I knew if Mom put on whatever it was, I'd be the one paying the price, so I immediately forbade her from ever wearing the maid outfit."

"Huh? That's just sad."

"I was so looking forward to your overblown reaction, Masato. Pity."

"I'm not doing it for your entertainment!"

Masato wasn't stupid. He'd learned from his experience, developed defensive instincts, and taken preemptive actions. "Boring!" "Hopes dashed." "I wanted Mama to match us, too…" "Does no one care about my feelings?" Masato's survival was on the line here. This was the way it had to be.

And so Mamako looked just like she always did.

"Maid Wise, Maid Medhi, and Maid Porta. You are all adorable. I love it so much!"

"Mwa-ha-ha, thank you, thank you very much."

"Much obliged… Although personally, I would have loved to have you join us, Mamako…"

"But I don't want to see Masato suffer! I can live without it!"

"Yes, well put, Porta! You're the best… And I think that's enough chatter about the costumes. Let's focus."

The five of them needed to figure out their goals for the day.

"Due to lack of personnel, we'll have to clear the tower another time. Shiraaase's handling the investigation…so what does that leave for us to do?"

"Clearly, we gotta do something about this ruin. Repair and clean it. Which is where us maids come in. Today we gotta be maids all day and focus on maid work."

"I'm not entirely sure remodeling buildings counts as maid work, but I do agree we should at least bring the place up to habitable levels."

"Leave that to my Item Creation! As long as I have the materials, I can fix this building or make it even more incredible!"

"I can't wait to see it, Porta. Well, everyone, today is the first day of Mom's Guild. Let's all work hard!"

"""""Right!"""""

With Mamako's pep talk, everyone pumped a fist high in the air and set to work.

Mamako and Wise saw them off.

"Take care out there! And you can relax and work at a comfy pace, if you like."

"That's what Mamako says, but we've got a mountain of work waiting for us, so don't forget that."

Masato, Medhi, and Porta were heading out.

"Okay, shopping team moving out! Anyone forgetting anything?"

"Shopping list, money… No, I'm ready."

"Off to town we go! I'm so excited!"

The party had split into the home guard team and the shopping team. Today's goal was to get the guild base repaired. This was an urgent mission of critical importance.

The shopping team was off to town to buy the building materials they needed. After saying good-bye to Mamako and Wise, they left the plateau the inn stood on.

"Okay, Porta, let's go!"

"Yes! I'm coming!"

Medhi took Porta's hand, and the two ran off happily. Masato smiled as he ambled along after them, gazing at the two maids as they headed into the… Hmm, wait.

An idea struck him.

"…Hey, Medhi, Porta. Assuming the two of you are heroines, shouldn't you be running off with me? Isn't that how it works?"

Medhi would grab Masato's arm, squeezing her quite noticeable chest against him as he turned bright red.

Porta would suddenly take his hand, urging him on like an innocent darling, bringing out all of Masato's brotherly instincts.

Yet, no such thing happened. Not even any hints it would happen.

"…Well, whatever. It was just a thought. Ha-ha."

With a hollow laugh, he looked up at the blue sky, wiping his eyes. He wasn't crying. These weren't tears.

On they walked, Medhi and Porta enjoying themselves, Masato wallowing in loneliness, until they reached the town.

The three of them headed down the main road lined with item and equipment shops. They breathed the salty sea breeze, with the faint lapping of the waves as background music.

It was still early, so there weren't that many people on the road yet. Porta spotted their target.

"Ah, there's a general goods store! I bet they'll have what we're looking for!"

"Porta's sensors are firing again! Come on, Masato!"

"Got it. Let's do this."

It was a big store, several times the size of the shops around it. Out front there were piles of wood and stone and gardening supplies.

Inside there were displays filled with daily necessities, furniture, even building walls and roofs.

"Wow, this is like a hardware store that's trying too hard. But it's definitely what we're after. Looks like they sell all the common item materials, so we could stock up on anything we're short of in that department, too. Never know when Amante might decide to bring the fight to us."

"Yes, she seems to view us as enemies," Medhi said, looking around. "She could very well attack at any moment."

One of the Four Heavenly Kings of the league of evil might just pop up in the town's general store...

"Nah."

"No way."

That would be ridiculous. What could possibly lead to that? There was no point worrying about it.

"Enough chitchat; let's buy some stuff!"

"Yes. We need materials to repair the guild base... Whaddaya say, Porta?"

"Yes! They have a lot of building materials! We can make Mom's Guild's base look amazing! Ahhhh! I'm so excited!"

The creative soul within her sparked, Porta could no longer restrain herself. "That wall and that roof... Oh, but that wall's nice, too!" Her eyes were darting all over the place, and she started scurrying here and there, to and fro. Totally forgetting the group.

It was adorable. So adorable it was impossible to think anything else.

"This is Porta's paradise. A paradise where we can sit and watch Porta frolic to our hearts' content."

"Guaaards! I've got your guy right here!"

"Not in a weird way! Stop yelling! ...Not that anyone's coming..."

"Um, sir?"

"Whoa, they actually did?!"

The voice came from behind him. Was he about to be arrested? Like, actually arrested? Shaking in his boots, a drop of cold sweat running down his brow, he turned...

It wasn't a security guard. It was a woman wearing an apron with the store's logo. If he were to be rude enough to guess her age, he'd guess that she was probably in her forties. And a little on the plump side.

The moment Masato saw her friendly smile, a light bulb went off in his mind. "Oh, she's a mother," he whispered to himself.

He was instantly convinced of it. As certain as he'd ever been of anything. He'd immediately identified the pack of women at the town entrance as mothers, but this was even more obvious.

He knew for sure this lady was someone's mo—

"Um, Masato? What are you...?"

"Huh? ...Oh...!"

When Medhi poked him, he finally snapped out of it.

Immediately declaring any woman he sees a mother? What? That made no sense. It was just dumb. He was embarrassing himself.

Surprised by this response, the woman laughed—at him. Gah.

"Tee-hee, that certainly wasn't the response I expected! But you're right. I am a mother... Although I'm surprised you could tell."

"Huh? ...Oh, uh... Yeah, I dunno, it just came to me."

"No, this is clearly your special power, Masato! Your hero power allows you immediately discern if someone is a mother or not! ...Just kidding. Heh-heh."

"Medhiiiiii!! Quit saying random stuff like thaaaat!! No way that's the case here...right? It's not true, right? Tell me it isn't!"

It would really suck if she wasn't joking. Like, seriously suck. Think about it...

Masato, the boy brought into the game world with his mother.

A boy designated a hero, yet his mother outdid him in strength, leadership, and anything else imaginable.

And his unique power allowed him to identify if someone was a mother or not.

Where would that leave him?

If that was the case...who even was he? What was the point of him at all?

No. It can't be true... Please, someone tell me it isn't...

This was like a saint discovering they had a natural affinity for evil, only like, a hundred times more painful and depressing. It left him practically catatonic.

But then someone called out to the mom storekeeper.

"You there! I'm looking for washboards and laundry detergent. How about some help over here?"

This arrogant request came from a brusque girl with her hair tied back in a ponytail. She wore light armor and had a black coat slung over her shoulders. At her hip was a thin sword, and in her hands were shopping baskets filled to the brim with toilet paper.

It was Amante.

"*Sigh...* With this many people, securing the necessary supplies is a real chore... Oh, right. I need to buy some compresses for myself. Gotta treat my butt and shin... Huh?"

At this point, Amante saw Masato's group staring at her, and her eyes narrowed. "W-wait a minute!" She hastily hid the toilet paper nearby, sealing away the mundaneness of it.

A sinister aura billowed forth as she turned her scornful gaze to Masato's group once again.

"You're Mamako Oosuki's son and companions! To think we would meet in a place like this... Shopping, are you? Goodness, don't you have anything better to do?"

"You're doing the exact same thing, you know."

"Um, Masato, she hit her butt and shin on the stairs yesterday, and it sounds like she's trying to get treatment now, but it's far too late and they're both going to have a nasty bruise. Poor thing."

"Y-you there, maid! That's a horrible assumption to make! Now you've got me very concerned!!"

Apparently, that was not a matter girls could treat lightly. Amante looked seriously ready to cry.

But she did her best to recover and plastered a villainous grin across her face.

"A-anyway! My body never bruises! And bruises vanish in time! ...More importantly, let me tell you something—"

"No, they won't vanish. You'll have those bruises forever, and then

you'll lose all confidence in your body. From this point on, every time you see your butt or shin, you'll heave a very sad sigh. You poor thing."

"Unh... *Sniff...* Wahhhh!"

Medhi was a little too merciless, and Amante really did burst into tears.

"M-Medhi! I think that's enough! For your own sake, dial it down."

"*Tch,* all right." The sheer venom of her dark power threatened to permanently ruin Medhi's image. He had to stop her.

"See, Amante? It's okay now. If you have something to tell us, we're listening. Go ahead."

"*Hic!* I don't care anymore! I've got nothing to tell you now! There's no point! I mean, we're enemies!"

"Sure, we seem to be... But that aside, go ahead and just blab everything like you did yesterday. You're dumb enough to do that, right?"

"I'm not dumb! ...Gah... I've had enough! You can't make me say it no matter what you do! I'm never telling you I called in a hit on your base!"

"Huh? A hit?"

Apparently, not only had Amante decided Masato and his party were her enemies for no good reason, but she'd also already gone and started attacking the Mom's Guild castle.

This might actually be serious... No, that was just a passing fancy.

Hmm... But Mom's there, so it won't be a problem.

If they were attacking the guild base, they'd just wind up answering to Mamako's overpowered abilities. He didn't know what form Amante's hit would take, but no matter who showed up, they never stood a chance. Mamako would win easily, and Masato would never get to lift a finger. It would go down just the way it always did.

Masato looked tense for like, a second, and then let out a long sigh, regaining his calm.

But then...

"Masato! Medhi! Porta! If you're in here, answer me!"

...Wise's voice suddenly echoed through the room. She was supposed to be guarding the fort with Mamako...

Masato turned toward the front door and saw a maid on a rampage, clutching her frilly skirt tight—Maid Wise. "Ah! There you are!" Wise spotted them and came racing over.

"Whoa, what the heck? Why are you here—?"

"Talk later! Right now, you've gotta hurry back to base! It's real bad over there! At this rate, Mamako might actually lose!"

"...Huh?"

Mamako? Lose?

Those were two words that had never before gone together. The very concept made Masato's brain shut down. "Don't just stand there! Medhi, Porta, grab hold of me!" "R-right!" "Everyone's here!" Wise grabbed Masato's arm, shot Amante some side-eye, and then activated a teleport spell...

The four of them were back at the plateau on the edge of town, right outside the ruined inn.

"Come on! Hurry! To Mamako!"

"O-okay!"

Wise gave him a push, and Masato broke into a run.

He was definitely worried now.

No way... How it is it even possible for her to lose?!

It wasn't. There was no way it could be. But as hard as it was to believe, Wise's desperation definitely made it seem like the impossible was really happening.

"Augh... Mom!"

Hoping she was still unharmed, he burst into the inn. And there...

...he found Mamako in the entrance hall wearing an apron over her usual clothing. This was cleaning-style Mamako, equipped with a bandanna tied around her head to protect it from dust and splashes.

In front of her was a crystal ball the size of an infant, along with a strange person who had a hood pulled over their eyes. From their size, it was most likely a male—a well-built one.

What was going on here?

"Like I said, ma'am, simply placing this crystal ball here guarantees customers will flock to the place. They'll just keep coming one after the other! Amazing, right?"

"Th-that's true… If we had that, all kinds of people would come here, and our guild would grow in no time…"

"It certainly would! I guarantee it. Every guild needs one of these. But, ma'am, this offer is only good today. It's a special discounted price that won't be seen again for quite some time."

"I see… Today only…"

"So I'm telling you, ma'am, you don't have time to think about it. You need to make up your mind right now!"

Once Masato heard this exchange, he knew.

That explained it.

Of all the things this could be… A door-to-door salesman, reeeee-ally…?

Yep. A salesman here to sell her something she didn't need.

All that worrying for this… Masato felt like a total idiot. Argh.

He also felt incredibly embarrassed for yelling "Augh… Mom!" and bursting in there. Ugh.

"…Hey, Wise. Gimme your head. I need to smack it."

"Hey! Why do I have to get hit?! This is serious here! …Ah, look!"

Wise frantically pointed to the scene unfolding between Mamako and the salesman.

"Oh, that's right, you said you were adventuring with your son? Then you'll have to buy this. I'm sure your son would be delighted with this purchase!"

"Ma-kun would be delighted? …Okay, I'll pay whatever you ask!"

Mamako took out her wallet. For Masato's happiness, no price was too steep.

"See! If they just bring you up, Mamako will lose instantly! I saw this threat coming and came running! I was totally right!"

"Uh, well… Fair. You were right to be concerned…"

But this was nothing like what he'd imagined. This was so different. So very, very different.

But he definitely needed to stop it.

"*Sigh*… All right."

He'd leave Wise's punishment for later. He stepped forward.

Rudeness worked best in situations like this. Masato just placed himself right between Mamako and the salesman.

"Uh, if you'll excuse me."

"Oh, Ma-kun! Everyone! Perfect timing! This man—"

"Yeah, yeah, I get it. He's a pushy salesman. Thanks very much," Masato said, greeting the man sarcastically.

The salesman's smile froze. This guy had rather stern features for his line of work. He looked more like a local thug. Kinda intimidating...

But Masato wasn't about to lose here. If he showed any signs of weakness, they'd end up buying the thing. He needed to push this guy right out.

"So, Mr. Pushy Salesman. I'm gonna have to ask you to leave. I don't need you selling your useless crap to my mother."

"No, no, nooo, my boy. I assure you, it is *not* useless! Our products are genuine rare items, and they work exactly as described—"

"You don't say? Then you won't mind if we verify that... Porta, got a moment?"

"Okay! Leave it to me!"

Porta came trotting forward and looked the crystal ball over. "Hmmm... This is..." Porta had the Appraise skill, and her judgment was always correct. If this was some dime-store glass sphere, she'd know right away...and that's precisely what Masato expected.

But Porta suddenly started shaking and looked up at Masato with panic in her eyes.

"Uhhhhh, M-M-M-Maaasato! Masatoooo!"

"What is it, Porta? You're even cute when you panic."

"Th-thank you? N-no, th-th-this... This is..."

"This is?"

"A bomb! A bomb big enough to blow the whole inn uuuuup!"

"Huh? A bomb? ...One big enough to blow up the... WHAAAAAT?!"

He didn't want to believe it, but Porta was never wrong.

This crystal ball actually was a powerful bomb.

"Duuuude!! Why the hell would you try to sell us something like that?! Take this thing outta... Uh, what? Where'd he go?!"

There was no sign of the salesman. He must have booked it while they were distracted by the bomb.

The crystal ball began to glow—a pulsing red light accompanied by a screeching noise that clearly spelled danger.

Was this the countdown starting?

Everyone went pale.

"Uh… Uh-oh… Is it gonna explode?! Are we about to get blown up?!"

"Masato, do something! Now!"

"Do what?! …Uh…uh…"

"Pick up the bomb and jump into the ocean with it, Masato! That will save *us*, at the very least! Go on, Masato! Be our hero!"

"Right, got it! …Wait, why do I have to jump in with it?! Can't I save myself, too? Can't I just throw it in the ocean?! That way—"

"Ah! It's flashing faster! It's about to blowwwww!"

"WHAAAAT?! E-everyone, run for iiiiit!!"

The crystal bomb was at its limit. It could explode at any second. There was nothing that could be done but try to get outside the blast zone.

Then…

"Hmm… Oh, I know. Okay!"

Mamako suddenly sat down next to the crystal bomb.

She then put it on her knees, wrapping it in a warm embrace.

"Come now, don't cry. Mommy's right here, so it'll all be okay. There, there. Who's a good boy?"

Soothing tones, gentle rubs, there theres. Like she was quieting a fussy child.

Masato couldn't comprehend what he was seeing.

"Wha…? Mom?! What are you doing?! What in the—?!"

"I'm comforting it, of course! …This bomb was throwing a tantrum like a little baby, right? So I just thought if Mommy held it, it might settle down."

"There's no way that'll work!! You can't soothe a bomb—!"

Or at least, you shouldn't be able to.

But as Mamako patted the crystal's back, the flashing and siren slowed, and the crystal bomb grew silent. "Um…seriously?" Seriously. It was completely safe once more.

The surface of the crystal bomb was peaceful, like the face of a baby that had fallen asleep in its mother's arms.

What had happened? There was only one answer.

This was another special mom skill—**A Mother's Soothing**.

"When a baby starts crying, you give it a hug and soothe it. Then they'll quiet down real quick. I used to do that with you, Ma-kun. Hee-hee. This brings back memories."

"Um, w-wait a sec. That only works on babies... You're hugging a bomb, Mom..."

"That's true, but to mothers, there's not much difference between a bomb and a baby. They both just erupt out of nowhere and cause a huge fuss... If you think of it that way, bombs are actually pretty adorable! Hee-hee-hee."

"Uh, no, bombs are definitely *not* adorable..."

A mother's love could allow her to treat even an explosive like her own child, and that proved every bit as effective as a bomb disposal squad... Yeah, that doesn't make any sense.

Still, this was how Mamako operated.

Mamako's actions had once again saved the day, and now it was noon.

Electing to eat lunch somewhere with a nice view, they'd carried the board outside the inn and placed it on some stones of the right height. Mamako lined up some handmade sandwiches on it, and everyone was enjoying lunch.

Mamako was sitting next to Masato. Too close for comfort.

"Ma-kun, you were so cool back there. When you burst in to save Mommy and the way you fought that salesman. It was wonderful! You're Mommy's hero, Ma-kun."

"Ugh... I'm the sort of hero who fights only duplicitous salesmen... That's my only accomplishment..."

"Oh, I know! I want you to eat this sandwich, Ma-kun. I think it's the best of all the ones I made today. Can I feed it to you? Say, 'Ah!'"

"Geez, knock that off! You're getting carried away! If you don't stop that right now, I'm gonna have to get angry!"

"Oh my. Ma-kun's ready to explode. I'll have to use A Mother's Soothing on you. Come on, Ma-kun. Into my arms!"

"Please stop! Just let me eat like a normal person!"

Saving her from the pushy salesman caused her to cling to Masato like a grateful heroine. This was far too much, and he was getting extremely annoyed.

Masato considered forcefully pushing her away, but...

"Listen, Masato. Mamako really saved us back there, so maybe she deserves a little reward? At least let her soothe you." *Smirk.*

"I agree. Letting her soothe you is the best way to show your gratitude. Right here in front of all of us." *Grin.*

"Mama's soothing looks so relaxing!" *I'm jealous!*

The maids across the table were all in favor of it. Porta looked genuinely envious, but the other two were clearly malicious, urging Masato to let Mamako dote on him out of sheer spite.

Well, he could answer that call...in their dreams. Letting his mother soothe him was completely out of the question.

Time to forcefully change the subject!

"Oh, hey! This is no time to talk about ridiculous crap! We've got more important things to worry about!"

"Huh? Like what? I can't imagine what could be more important than this."

"No, really! Like that salesman from earlier!"

That lunatic had tried to sell them a bomb. That alone was worth discussing...and there was one other reason to do so.

"C'mon, Medhi. You remember, right? What Amante said?"

"Oh, now that you mention it... She did say she'd called in a hit on our base. You mean...she was talking about that salesman?"

"That's what I'm thinking. And I'm pretty sure I'm right..."

Before Masato could say another word, Mamako leaned in against him.

"Oh? Ma-kun, you all met Amante again? Where? What does this talk about a hit mean?"

"Ah, yeah, I guess I did see her in the store. I was in such a hurry I didn't really register it... Porta, can you fill me in?"

"Huh? ...U-um... S-sorry! I'm not quite sure..."

"Porta was busy poring over what the store had to offer, so I'm not surprised she never noticed. I'll bring everyone up to speed..."

But before he could...

"I really don't see why you need to explain that you happened to bump into me in the general store buying up all the toilet paper like a frumpy housewife."

...another voice explained what happened. He turned to look.

Speak of the devil. Amante was walking up the path to the plateau.

"What...are you doing here?"

"Does it matter? There's no reason I should have to tell you that I came to check because the explosion never happened."

"Yep, she's definitely the kind of idiot who just explains everything at the slightest prompting. So useful!"

"What?! You there, maid! You will not call me an idiot again! I'm not a useful idiot, I'm—!"

"Can I ask a question? You mentioned you'd called in a hit. Was that the salesman from earlier?"

"Hmph. Naturally it was, but that's no reason for me to answer honestly!"

"Sending us a bomb is mean! I don't like it!"

"What are you talking about? We're enemies, remember? I didn't know how to handle you in the tower and felt like you were too much for me, so why *wouldn't* I send you a bomb?"

"Now she's explaining stuff we didn't even ask about..."

Idiots were so useful. All the party had to do was let her ramble and they could squeeze all the info they needed out of her. Hard to see her as a serious threat, really.

Then Mamako stood up.

"Um, Amante, do you have a moment?"

"I told you, no matter what you ask me, I'll never answer... Eep! ...Mamako Oosuki?!"

The moment Mamako spoke to her, Amante's expression suddenly turned wary. She quickly took several steps back, then drew her sword.

But while Amante was all prepared to fight, Mamako just wanted to talk.

"Wait," Mamako said. "I have no intention of fighting you. I just want to ask you—"

"Stay away! Don't talk to me!"

"D-don't talk like that, now. Please. Just listen. All the adventurer children are gathered at your place, right? Their mothers are all worried about them, so I think they should come home soon—"

"Stay back! Stop talking! I refuse any contact with you!"

When Mamako took a step forward, Amante took a step back. When Mamako tried to speak, Amante shouted over her, adamant in her rejection.

Amante seemed pretty relaxed in her dealings with Masato and the maids but was clearly deathly afraid of Mamako. It was downright unnatural.

Amante kept backing away from Mamako before she finally turned on her heel and fled.

Masato hastily called after her, "W-wait! You can't keep showing up and then running away! Why'd you even come here? Was it just to check on us?"

"You can ask, but do you think I'll be nice enough to answer? I came to tell you the next hit was already in motion, but now I'm not gonna bother!"

"Huh? ...The next hit...?!"

But no sooner had the words left his mouth...

...than a loud noise echoed from the ruined inn. A loud crash, like something massive falling over.

"*Tch!* What now?! ...I'll go check it out."

Masato turned to run off. "Wait up!" "It's dangerous to go alone!" "Let's all go!" His party called after him. He was their leader! Naturally, they were concerned for his well-being. This was wonderful, he thought, looking back.

"All right, Mamako, come on!"

"Mamako, hurry!"

"Mama! I'm all set! Give the order!"

"Thank you, everyone. Let's go!"

Everyone had gathered around Mamako. Yep, he should have known better. He'd had a hunch, at least.

He wanted to curl up in a ball and cry, but this was an emergency. "Pfft, this happens all the time," Masato snorted and ran off. Not crying. Definitely not crying.

*   *   *

By the time they reached the ruined inn, the entrance was already a disaster.

"Wow, what happened?!"

"Oh my! What a fright!"

The front door had been smashed in, and pieces of it were everywhere. The walls had already been crumbling, but now there was nothing left of them, only the support pillars remaining.

The culprits were in plain sight. Ten rough-hewn roustabouts, clearly all muscle brained but also definitely formidable, cackled in guttural tones.

One of the thugs stepped forward: a man with a Mohawk and the biggest muscles. He glared at them, snarling...and Masato recognized him.

"Hey! You're the salesman!"

"That's right! Thank you for your patronage... Ha! Heh-heh-heh."

Clearly, this was his true form. The way he spoke now matched his general vibe.

"Yo, we're takin' over. We're with the Libere Rebellion... Not like we need to tell you that, though."

"So you're Amante's minions?!"

"That's right. I'm glad you understand. I may have messed up earlier, but this time we'll get the job done... 'Ey, you guys!"

"You got it, Pocchi! Let's smash this place up!"

"Smaaaashhhhhhhh! Bwa-ha-ha-ha-ha-ha!"

At Pocchi's orders, the hoodlums began to rampage. They swung their swords and axes around, attacking the remaining pillars and the stairs.

This was no time for standing and gawking. They had to stop this. Masato drew his sword and got ready to charge in.

"Hey! Stop that, or we'll—!"

"You'll what, kid? Fight us? Bad idea. You lay a finger on us, it'll just make things worse."

"Worse how?"

"Like this."

Pocchi took a piece of paper and a small crystal out of his pocket. "Right, first, like this..." he muttered and then pressed his thumb into the crystal.

As he did, there was a huge explosion behind Masato's group. "Wha...?!" He spun around and saw a huge pillar of water shoot up from the ocean. The water flung skyward by the explosion's force came raining down.

"W-wait...?!"

"Just a little demonstration. That's what happens when you use the crystal bombs we showed you earlier... And we've got them placed all over town."

"Huh?! Hang on, you're kidding, right?"

"Bombs that powerful are all over town?!"

"Whoaaa... Wh-wh-wh-what do we do?! Mama!"

"I—I don't know... I suppose w-we'll have to go find them all and soothe them..."

"No, no, Ms. Mamako. There are twenty of them! Evem with your weird power, you'll never make it in time. After all, I've got the trigger right here! Heh-heh."

He rolled the crystal trigger around on his hand, threatening to press it at any moment. Thoroughly savoring his advantage.

"So that's the deal. You get it now? We don't care either way, but if you don't wanna see the town get blown to bits, you'd better mind your manners. Got it? Do ya?"

"*Tch...* All right."

These guys had control. Hasty resistance would be foolish. He had no choice. Masato sheathed his sword, demonstrating his lack of resistance.

The others also made it clear they weren't about to fight. They all moved behind Masato, using him as a shield. "Ugh, *now* you guys rely on me..." But he was secretly rather pleased.

"...So what's your goal here?"

"Simple. We got orders from the top to go hog-wild here. We can do whatever we want! And believe me, we will... Heh-heh-heh. Let's start by having your little maids take orders from their new masters."

That was definitely a skeevy smile on Pocchi's face. And his request was...!

*   *   *

In the dining hall.

"First, we eat! Doesn't matter what, just bring us some grub! And be quick about it!"

Nobody cared about the state of the place. "Faster!" "Chop-chop!" They just sat down anywhere, yelling for food.

The kitchen was bustling.

"Damn them! What's with those guys? What kind of villain demands food?"

"Masato! I know how you feel, but if you've got time to grumble, get those hands moving! Chop those ingredients up! Then break and scramble those eggs!"

"They've got bombs all over town! We have to do what they say!"

"Will it be good? It'll be good! A good item...done! Wise, here you go! The frying pan's all ready!"

"Thanks, Porta! That's a huge help!"

Masato's party was cooking—all of them, with not nearly enough equipment, making whatever they could as quickly as they could.

But they were missing one member.

"Geez, where'd Mom go? This is her specialty!"

"She said she had to get something ready! I think she's preparing something for the meal, but...!"

Wise got her dish done first.

"Okay, all done! Schoolgirl eggs!"

It was just eggs, scrambled and fried. They were only slightly burnt, but that was part of the charm.

She stuck them on a plate and ran over to Pocchi with them.

"Right, here you are! It would be a disgrace to let thugs like you have Mamako's cooking! Eat this and scram!"

"Mm? Eggs? Eh. Whatever, I'll eat it."

Pocchi took a bite. How was it?

"Mm... Super whatever. Neither good nor bad. Totally average."

"A-average is just fine by me! Quit gripin' and eat!"

"Huh? Get real, lady. We ain't eatin' anything that ain't at least good. Next!"

"Grrr!"

Wise couldn't make anything except eggs that were neither good nor bad, so she retreated. Shame.

Medhi's dish was finished next.

"Whew, all done. This should make short work of them."

She certainly seemed confident. There was a satisfied smile on her lips.

Her plate had something green and purple with gooey bits of dark brown—"Whoa, don't you dare even try to serve that!"—which was rejected before she even brought it to him.

"B-but...it's a shame to waste food..."

Medhi was crestfallen. A shadow crossed her face, and she turned to the wall, thumping her foot against it. "Wah, Medhi?!" "Stop, the building's damaged enough!" They forced her to rein in the dark power.

But Medhi was still very disappointed.

"...I put so much work into it, and they wouldn't even try it..."

"It was a good plan, Medhi. Shame it didn't work."

"Yeah. Evil Medhi strikes again! Your scheme to polish them all off by making them eat that nightmare dish was this close to succeeding!"

"Huh? Scheme? No, I wasn't...! I just tried to cook the best thing I could and hoped they'd enjoy it!"

""Uh...""

Apparently, that Mysterious Object X had been Medhi's best effort. "...Wise." "Mm, got it." Masato and Wise formed a silent pact to never let Medhi cook again.

That was all the time they could spare on consolation.

"Where's the next dish? Keep 'em coming! Do you wanna see the town explode or what?" Pocchi roared.

"Damn! We've gotta make something else!" Wise's was too normal, Medhi's unacceptable. That left Masato to make some man-cooking from what he half remembered his mom doing.

But then, the star of the show appeared.

"Sorry it took me so long! I'll get right down to cooking!"

"Geez, finally! Hurry up and... Uh... Huh?"

Mamako came running into the kitchen, and Masato's eyes widened in horror.

Just like the teenage girls, she was wearing a frilly maid dress. Her bust was just too large for it, and she'd been forced to leave the top largely unbuttoned, and the skirt was much too short so that every time she bent over, her excessively skimpy panties were easily seen.

A moment after he laid eyes on his mom the maid, Masato heard the sound of every last cell in his brain detonating. *Pop, pop, pop, pop, pop, pop, pop, pop,* and then *bzzzt.*

"Are you trying to kill meeeeeeee?!"

"Huh?! N-no, I would never! Ma-kun, calm down!"

"How can I be calm?! Why are you dressed like a maid?!"

"Why? ...B-because Mr. Pacchi—"

"Pacchi? My name's Pocchi! Get it right!"

"Oh, sorry... Mr. Pecchi here said he wanted the maids to serve him, so Mommy just thought she was supposed to get changed, too—"

"You don't need to do whatever Pucchi says! Geez!"

"No, listen, my name's Picchi. Wait, I mean, Pocchi. Geez... And by the way, Ms. Mamako..." Pocchi looked Mamako over from head to toe, sneering. "Well, you're young and beautiful, so it don't look bad on you or nothin'. But a mom in maid clothes? Pfft. Are all moms this dumb?"

Pocchi was part of the Libere Rebellion. They opposed the very concept of parents, so naturally he didn't have much respect for Mamako.

"Hey, knock it off."

But Masato was not about to let it go unchallenged.

Pocchi hadn't said anything wrong. Even her son thought Mamako's outfit was ridiculous.

But that didn't mean he was about to let a total stranger say so.

Masato and Pocchi glared fiercely at each other.

"Now, now, Masato. I don't like that look in your eyes. You forgetting I got the trigger right here?"

"No, I remember. You'll have to excuse me."

"I'm glad we understand each other... Now get your dumb-looking mom to make us some grub—although I'm sure she can't make anything but dumb food, heh-heh."

"Grrr..."

He reeeeeally wanted to punch Pocchi. Or grab a fistful of his Mohawk and yank it out.

But if he could silence the thug's tongue with cooking? That would be even better.

"Mom! I'm gonna let the fact that you're wearing the maid outfit slide! So, please!"

"Okay, got it! I'll do the best cooking I can!"

Mamako took over the run-down kitchen.

"Ma-kun! What ingredients do we have?"

"Leftovers from breakfast, eggs, and some random vegetables! They're all chopped up!"

"In that case... Porta! Can I get a wok?"

"Okay! ...Will it be good? It'll be good! A good item...done!"

"Wise, can you use your magic to start the fire? I need a nice strong flame!"

"Got it! ...*Spara la magia per mirare... Fuoco Fiamma!*"

"Medhi, can you get the plates ready?"

"Sure! I can help cook as well, but for now I'll focus on getting the plates out!"

Mamako even knew exactly how to handle Medhi. This was her domain.

It was done in a jiff!

"Hee-hee, all ready! Mommy's special fried rice!"

One of the quickest dishes around. Mamako heaped the fried rice onto the plate and rushed it over to Pocchi.

"Here you go! It's hot, so be careful."

"Oh, come on! Fried rice? That's some lazy cooking right there. You just throw the thing in a pan and it's done! I swear, moms are—"

"Now, now, don't say that. Why don't you try it? I think you'll like it!"

"Like it? ...W-well, it does smell pretty good... The rice isn't sticking together at all, and it looks perfectly cooked... *Gulp...* R-right, guess I'll just have a taste."

Pocchi picked up the oversized spoon and shoved a heaping pile of rice into his mouth.

He was astonished.

"Th-this... This isn't just any fried rice... Th-there's ham in it!"

"That's right! I like it best with fried pork, but sadly I didn't have any, so I had to use ham instead. How is it?"

"Ham fried rice... Y'know, my own mom used to make that a lot... Pork is expensive, so ham's good enough, she always said... What am I even saying...?"

Misting up a little, Pocchi kept eating. "Hey! Only Pocchi gets some?! No fair!" "I'm hungry, too!" "Coming right up!" The other ruffians got their portions one after the other, and the result:

"""""...Dang... This reminds me of my mom's fried rice..."""""

All the thugs were staring off into the distance, remembering their old homes.

Mamako's ham fried rice proved super effective.

"All the fuss they were making, and now they're just eating Mom's fried rice in silence... Mom strikes again. That's what her food does."

"You want food, you go to Mamako. It's not that I suck at it!"

"Very true... I'll have to have her teach me and make some for everyone..."

""Please don't!"" *Grin.*

A new threat was in the offering, but at least they'd managed to meet Pocchi's demands. Masato's party was relieved...

...but just then...

"Yo, yo, don't think this is over yet, kids. That's just the prelim! Our rampage is only getting started! Now that our bellies are full, next... Heh-heh-heh... What do you think?"

"Ack... What now?"

Masato looked cautious, and Pocchi grinned, oblivious to the piece of ham stuck to the side of his face...

In the baths.

"Now it's bath time! Get this bath full!"

With not a care for the horrifying state of the baths, Pocchi and his roustabouts had discarded their equipment and clothing, totally ready for a soak—and were demanding the bath be filled.

Masato's party was at a loss.

"The bath itself is so broken it won't even hold water…"

"And even if it did, we can't get cold water to come out of the taps… We can't exactly escort this crowd to the inn we bathed at yesterday…"

"If we had the repair materials, I could do something about it, but… without those, I can't help…"

"Right… And once again, Mom is nowhere to be found…"

Wherever she'd gone, Masato, Medhi, and Porta had no idea what to do.

"Ha-ha! Then this is my time to shine!" Wise declared with utter confidence. She seemed to have a plan…

Oh, right. Wise can use magic.

"Leave this to me! First… *Spara la magia per mirare… Pietra Muro!* And! *Pietra Muro!*"

Wise chain cast. Two wide stone walls appeared opposite each other.

"Here comes another! …*Spara la magia per mirare… Pietra Muro!* And! *Pietra Muro!*"

Two more walls appeared. They lined up with the first two, forming a square.

And she wasn't done casting.

"And for the finish! …*Spara la magia per mirare… Alto Acqua Sfera!* And! *Bomba Fiamma!*"

A surge of water and a powerful fire appeared inside the stone walls, and a ton of steam rose off the top.

Ta-da! The magic bath was complete.

"Mwa-ha-ha. Well? Whaddaya think? …Pocchi, was it? Hop on in there already."

"Normally, I'd teach you a lesson on manners here…but right now, I'm really jonesin' for a bath."

Pocchi stepped up on the wall and was about to dive in…

…when a moment later, the walls and water vanished into thin air.

"Ow! Hey! Where'd it go? What's the meaning of this?!"

"I—I don't know! …What happened?!" Wise seemed every bit as surprised as Pocchi.

But honestly, Masato's group had seen this coming.

"Hmm… Well, it *was* magic."

"Wise was using attack spells. The effects of those never last for long, so of course it vanished."

"Um… I think we actually talked about this yesterday and decided not to make a bath with magic for that exact reason!"

"What?! We did?!"

They had indeed. Masato considered presenting Wise with an award for most useless Sage, but…

…now was not the time. Pocchi was absolutely livid.

"Yo, yo, yo! That was a dirty trick! Get this bath ready now! We've been holed up in that tower for ages with no baths! We're dyin' for a soak! Do you want us blowin' up the entire town?! Do ya?!"

Pocchi flashed the trigger crystal for the crystal bombs. The other riffraff took the hint and started kicking the walls of the bathroom, making threats. "H-hold on a minute—we'll do something!" Masato yelled, but he had no idea what that something might be.

Just then:

"Sorry it took so long!"

Mamako came running in. She still had that maid outfit equipped. Maid Mom.

"The dishes just took ages to get clean… It really is so inconvenient not having running water in the kitchen…"

"I can see how that would be tough… But, uh, Mom… Now they want a bath…"

"Oh my. We need to get a bath ready? Then… Oh, I know!"

Mamako drew Terra di Madre, the Holy Sword of Earth. "Wh-what, you want some?!" Pocchi's group scrambled for their gear, but Mamako had not drawn her weapon for battle.

Mamako lowered the tip of the sword and whispered, "O Mother Earth… If you're a mother, too, then you know how I feel… The bath isn't ready… We have to do something… If you understand how I feel, please, lend me your power!"

With that, she swung the sword upward.

The earth responded to Mamako's request. In an instant, the remains of the bath were pulled underground, replaced by a large bath made of natural stone.

A moment later, milky white liquid began burbling up into it—a hot spring.

A hot spring of that color? That smell? Masato had experienced this before.

"Wait… This is the stuff from Maman Village!"

"Oh, it is! Maman's Warm Milk, was it?"

"Uh, you don't have to say the name out loud… B-but the point is!"

Pocchi's group would finally be sated. Masato turned to look.

"Wh-what the…? I dunno what just happened. You're just using store-bought minerals to trick us… But, eh, we might as well get in."

The abrupt appearance of the hot spring seemed to have confused them, but Pocchi cautiously stepped in anyway. He slowly lowered himself in until his shoulders were covered.

He let out a long breath, and an expression of bliss spread across his face.

"Ooh… That's the stuff… And this really is a hot spring… Y'know, my mom always wanted to go to a hot spring, but we never had the money, and she was always busy at work…so all she could ever do was buy packs of the hot spring minerals and pretend she'd really gone."

He'd grown rather wistful. "Hey! No fair only Pocchi gets to bathe!"

"We're coming in, too!" Pocchi's goons began jumping in one after another.

"""""…Ahh… Yeah, my mom used to buy hot spring minerals, too… Scattered some in the water and it just absorbed the moisture and got all balled up…"""""

They each started remembering their homes and getting wistful as well.

Mamako's hot spring was super effective. On Mamako, too.

"That's so true… You think it'll dissolve eventually, but it never really does… I've made the same mistake." *Ho-hum.*

"Nobody cares, Mom. We don't need you getting wistful over hot spring minerals, too! …But once again, you've totally saved the day. Now…"

At last we're safe, Masato thought.

But Pocchi just glared at him.

"Yo, yo, you think this is over yet? The next bit is the main course! We've eaten, and we've taken a bath. What happens after that? Whaddaya think we'll ask for next?"

"Huh? ...Dinner, a bath, and then... N-no!"

"Heh-heh-heh. Looks like you got it... C'mon, boys! To the bedrooms!"

""""""Awww, yeah! I've been waitin' for this!"""""""

The time had finally come. The rabble all stood up, their expressions those of slobbering beasts. They went stampeding out of the bath.

Dinner. Bath. Only one thing followed those...

Pocchi was walking down the hall to the bedrooms, a bath towel wrapped around his waist and a skeevy smile on his lips.

"Now then, let's have that young pretty mom of yours give us lots of service...in bed! Heh-heh-heh! I can't wait."

"Hey! Wait! I said wait!"

"Hold it right there! Seriously, don't make Mamako do anything weird!"

"We'll have to stop you by force! It's the only way!"

"Yes! I've got a special item saved just for this!"

"Whoa, better not try anything. Did you forget we've got bombs hidden all over town? I left that trigger switch with one of my men. Anything happens to me, kaboom! Heh-heh-heh."

"Grr...!"

They were desperate to stop Pocchi but couldn't. They were helpless.

And they were already at the bedroom door.

"Now, lets see if she's ready... Wow, this room's a mess, but not bad, not bad."

Pocchi pushed Masato out of the way and stepped inside. The bed was nicely made.

And there was Mamako, smiling, a little unsure of herself.

"Mom... Why didn't you just run for it...? I told you to run for it!"

"Ma-kun, this is for the best. The lives of the villagers depend on it! I can't just run away."

"That sure sounds noble and everything, but…"

"Hee-hee, you're all worried about me, Ma-kun. I knew you loved me!"

"No, that's not the point!"

"I-it isn't? …Now Mommy's sad." *Sniffle.*

"Don't get depressed! Love's got nothing to do with it, anyone would be worried!"

"Yeah, that's enough of that. If we listen to all the protests of a son who's ashamed of his feelings, we'd be here all night. I can't wait any longer! Let's get this started!"

Pocchi pushed past Masato again. The time had finally come.

Pocchi flopped down on his back on the bed and gave Mamako a saucy wave.

"All right, Ms. Mamako. Time for a li'l service. Make it good. Heh-heh-heh."

"Very well."

"No! Wait—!"

"You shut your trap! If you're a real man, you'll grit your teeth and watch your mom debase herself!"

"Argh… Dammit… You can't…!"

Ignoring the look of anguish on Masato's face, Mamako slowly walked past him. He raised a hand listlessly but couldn't bring himself to stop her.

Mamako knelt down by the side of the bed.

"'Ey, Ms. Mamako, I don't need to tell you what to do, do I?"

"No, I know… All right, then…"

Mamako reached out her hand…

…picked up the blanket, and laid it out on top of Pocchi.

"Pocchi, time for beddy-bye," she whispered sweetly. "Night-night, Pocchi. Sleep tight."

She patted the blankets, tucking him in for bedtime.

Um.

""Hey?! What are you doing?!"" Masato and Pocchi both yelled. "Let me say it!" "Uh, okay, go ahead." It did seem better for the man on the receiving end to air his grievances.

"Yo, yo, yo, Ms. Mamako, what are you doin'?"

"What else? A little mom service…in bed! Night-night, Pocchi!" *Pat, pat.*

"I'm not here for night-night! That's not what I meant by 'service' at all! I was going for somethin' a li'l more *mature*—!"

"Nighty-night, sleep tight." *Pat, pat.*

"I told you, that's not what I meant! …B-but…y'know, when I was a kid…and I couldn't sleep…my mom used to do this… Really takes me back… G'night…"

Pocchi fell asleep. The rough-looking, Mohawk-sporting roustabout was sleeping like a baby.

Then…

"Yo, yo, what're you doing, Pocchi?!"

"You let Ms. Mamako pat your blanket and put you to sleep? That's just pathetic!"

"But we won't be that easy! We'll get some *adult* service out of her yet!"

"You're tellin' me! Mwa-ha-ha-ha!"

The rest of the hooligans came filing in…

…only to end up in bed with blankets spread across them and lovingly patted.

"""""…Zzzzz… Mommy… Zzz…"""""

"Hee-hee. They're all sleeping like babies."

They'd all fallen right asleep.

The party found a map of the crystal bombs in town on one of the sleeping roustabouts and took that and the trigger with them to recover all the bombs safely.

Evening came.

Having slept soundly, Pocchi and his goons were lined up in front of the entrance, bowing to Mamako.

"Um… So, uh… Sorry for causing all that fuss."

"No, no, it was my pleasure… So what will you all do now? Are you going back to that tower?"

"Uh… No, I'm thinkin' I'll swing by home first. Not 'cause I miss my mom or nothin'… But it can't hurt to show my face. I basically ran away from home, so…she might be worried, y'know?"

"That's true. I think it's best you go home and show your mother how well you're doing."

"Uh, yeah. I will… And again, sorry for all the trouble."

"No, not at all."

Bowing their heads several times like reformed delinquents, Pocchi's group took their leave. Mamako saw them off with a big smile on her face.

Masato's party was left frowning after them, at a loss as to what else they should be doing.

But it did seem like Mamako had entirely solved that problem.

That night.

"Whew…"

The hectic day had left Masato exhausted, and he was soaking his weary body in the hot spring. This was definitely the way to end a day. The water was perfect. His body and soul were practically melting into it.

He found himself wanting to sing a little ditty like, "Lovely water, ah-ha-haaa!" but he managed to stop himself. Self-restraint.

There were others in the bath with him, after all. It would be impolite to disturb them.

"Ahhh… Big baths are so great… I lived in a tiny apartment in the real world, and the tub was suuuper cramped. I could never really stretch out in them, so this is real luxury…"

"You must have lived in a real dump, Wise. I lived in an upscale condo, and the baths were really quite large. Not this large, of course, but still…"

"Hey, Medhi, don't just call it a dump! I swear, you're getting more twisted by the day… I mean, you aren't wrong…"

"Ohhh… It's so big that I want to start swimming… It's so hard to stop myself…"

The girls seemed to be quite relaxed on the other side of that cloud of steam.

Wise scooped up a handful of water and splashed it on the back of her neck. It ran down her flushed skin, over her collarbone, and down her chest without encountering notable obstruction.

Medhi did the same move, but the effect couldn't be more different. The water running down her skin pooled in the valley between her obstructions, like a squad of water droplets rendezvousing in the designated valley location.

Porta, sandwiched between them, kept standing up and fanning herself with her hands, presumably trying to avoid overheating. "Whoa!" She hastily steadied the shoulder bag she had balanced on her head.

Yep. They were super relaxed.

Despite the fact that Masato was in here.

"...Um... Are you sure you're all okay with this? I mean, I hate to spoil a relaxing bath, but—"

"Mm? Whatever. I'm waaaay past caring about mixed bathing. I got used to it. Just don't look this way! Looking's off-limits."

"Baths are just something we all use together now!"

"Hee-hee. Yes, it's better if we're all together."

"O-oh, really? ...But this is Medhi's first time joining us, so..."

"I...am certainly somewhat embarrassed... But if I can't do what the others do, I'd feel left out. Hopefully I'll gradually get used to it and, in time, be the first to invite you to join us. So please, don't mind me."

"That whole 'always be number one' upbringing sure manifests itself in some surprising ways... But if you're all good with it, cool."

With Medhi's consent, Masato's secret title, Mixed Bath Creep Level 2, advanced to Mixed Bath Creep Level 3! How far can this title go?!

The girls were okay with it. Now all Masato had to do was keep a certain part of himself from getting too worked up. That was easier said than done...

"You know, Masato, it's not like we're your main concern, is it? I mean...look next to you."

"Uh, yeah..."

Masato risked a glance to his side, where Wise was pointing.

Mamako was sitting there, lost in thought. Two breast-shaped islands floated on the surface of the water—but her expression made it clear that her mind had sunk straight to the bottom.

He wasn't all that concerned about her, but it did seem like he should say something.

"Uh, Mom, what's on your mind? You're the one who called for our customary naked strategy session. If you need our help with something, go ahead and ask."

"Huh? Oh... Right... It's about Pocchi and his gang. There was one thing I was a little worried about..."

"Oh?"

"I wonder if they made it home safe."

"...Huh?"

That was what Mamako was so worried about? What a mom thing to do. Any mother would be worried, naturally.

Was it really worth worrying over? Annoyed, Masato was about to say so when...

"Pocchi and his group packed up their bags and went right home! A major blow to our numbers, and I'm quite vexed!"

...Amante's angry voice echoed through the bathroom.

As it did, the door to the baths slammed open, and Amante came striding in.

She had a bath towel wrapped around a body that clearly had more up top than Wise's but wasn't quite in Medhi's league. In one hand was a basket with a sponge and some shampoo. It was pretty obvious that she came for a bath. You could never tell by looking at her that this was a surprise appearance by the enemy boss!

Then Amante abruptly turned back to the changing room and hid behind the door, only her very red face peering around it.

"Yo. First you show up out of nowhere, then you suddenly hide... What gives?"

"What gives?! Isn't it obvious?! I'm only wearing a bath towel! I can't possibly stand in front of a boy dressed like that!"

"Huh? ...O-oh, right. Wow! A *normal* reaction!" He was impressed.

"I didn't intend for that to be surprising! A-and what are you all doing? You're all in the same bath?! I never...!"

Amante's reaction was entirely justified, but Wise and Medhi were having none of it.

"Yeah, yeah, I get your point, so don't even bother."

"More importantly, I'd like you to explain why you're here in the first place! Although I imagine you'll tell us without prompting in a moment."

"Ha! You underestimate me again! I'll never admit that I've actually been hiding and watching what was going on the whole time!"

"And you waited for your moment to attack...or whatever this is instead?"

"You're right. She *is* wearing a bath towel... Are you really just here to use our bath?"

"Even if that were the case, there's no reason why I should just admit it! Why should I have to reveal that since I've been living in a tower with no bath I've had to wash myself in the ocean and am dying for a proper soak?!"

"Whoa, you washed yourself with salt water? That's so bad for your skin! ...Come to think of it, the moment she entered, I did smell something salty..."

"Yes, she totally reeks of the sea... And look, there's definitely a nasty bruise on her shin! The toll on her complexion, the odor, those bruises... How far will you go in this assault on your femininity?"

"...*Sniff*... Y-you're all girls, too... You could stand to be a little less blunt... That's hitting way too close to home..."

It seemed the girls' merciless criticisms had dealt a serious blow to Amante's feelings. They might very well drive her away without really doing anything...

...But then Mamako spoke up.

"Amante, dear, do you mind?"

"*Sniff*... What else is there to say? ...Wait! *Gasp! Mamako Oosuki?!*"

Amante hastily dried her eyes and glared at Mamako. She really was super wary around her.

"How dare you, Mamako Oosuki! To not only defeat the assassins but convince them to go back home?! I can't believe it! You're the most dangerous mother of all!"

"Goodness, I'm not dangerous—"

"You are! You're the greatest threat to the actualization of our ideals there is! I'll let you off today, but you won't get off so easy next time! Prepare yourself!"

With that last line, Amante left the changing room... Oh, never mind, she's back.

"You can turn the lights out, but leave the water! Not like I'm gonna sneak in and use it later! I'm definitely not gonna do that, but just be sure you don't drain the bath! That's all!"

And with that urgent plea, Amante ran away.

Mom's Guild Daily Report

Occupation: Mommy Maid (just because!)
Name: Mamako Oosuki

Business Report:

First day for the Mom's Guild. Lots of people visited, and we were so busy! The thing that left the biggest impression on me was when I was about to buy something from a salesman. Just then, Ma-kun came bursting in and saved me in the nick of time! It seems Ma-kun really does care about me... I would love to write all day about how happy that made me, but the space for answers is just too small. Such a shame!

Other Notes:

Per Medhi's request, here's how to make ham fried rice.
For one serving, you will need: one bowl of cooked rice, one egg (whisked), two slices of ham, one green pepper, one-quarter of a green onion, salt and pepper to taste, one teaspoon of soy sauce, and two tablespoons of vegetable oil.
Directions: 1. Sauté the finely chopped peppers and onion. 2. Add the rice and slowly pour the whisked egg over it, stirring with chopsticks. 3. Add the ham, season to taste, and quickly finish over a high flame.

Member Comments:

There's lots of other things I'd like to say, but anyway, don't let Medhi read this recipe, kthx.

I already have, tho?

\(^o^)/ We're doomed.

The key to keeping the rice from clumping is to really work the rice and eggs with chopsticks!

Chapter 3 When Mothers Assemble, They Form a Combo. No, I'm Not Talking About a Puzzle Game. Something Actually Terrible.

The next day, at breakfast (as always).

The dining room was even more of a mess thanks to the hooligans' assault, but all it took was Mamako's home-cooked meal to turn it into a place of happiness. Everyone felt like they could face the challenges the day would bring.

Perhaps she'd sniffed out that happiness—Shiraaase had shown up first thing that morning and joined them for breakfast, exchanging information as they ate.

"Hey, Wise, pass the soy sauce."

"Mm, here."

"Thanks… So that's basically what happened yesterday. We were dealing with Amante's minions all day long. And in the end, like always, Mom took care of everything."

"Mamako managed to convince Libere Rebellion members to return to their homes? That is impressive, even for her. Well done."

"Not at all! I barely did a thing."

"No need for modesty. You were amazing! …Oh, Porta, you've got rice on your cheek."

"Oops! When did that get there?"

With much excitement, the Mom's Guild report concluded.

Now it was Shiraaase's turn.

"So how about you, Ms. Shiraaase?"

"I have nothing particularly remarkable to report… I put out requests to each branch of operations but was unable to uncover any infooormation on the situation in town or the league in question."

"Uh… What? But aren't you an admin? You didn't manage to find anything?"

"I find it hard to believe there's no information anywhere on your side."

"Wise, Medhi, I entirely agree. Anything happening within the game should have some form of data or infooormation we can obtain. Yet, none of that reached my ears… Which means…"

"It's being intentionally hidden?" Masato asked.

Shiraaase hesitated but nodded. "Yes, that seems to be a reasonable assumption. But for them to keep infooormation from me… I can't imagine what possible reason there could be for that."

"Hmm… I suppose it could be as simple as everyone else hating you…"

Masato should probably have not said that aloud.

Shiraaase gave him a long look. Her eyes were intense, but with a calm, quiet beauty as she stared daggers at him. It was terrifying.

"I—I was just kidding!" he said, desperately trying to take it back.

He couldn't read her expression at all.

"Well," she said, "I will eventually find a way to avenge that comment."

"Crap… I knew she was pissed…"

"But to appear like that without being able to infooorm you of a single piece of valuable intel would hardly make me worthy of my name. The one thing I did manage to overhear relates to the matter of increasing guild membership. Normally only test players and adventurer NPCs are able to join guilds, but this time…"

But before Shiraaase could finish…

"Good morning! Sorry to show up this early. Is anyone here?"

…a woman's voice called from out the front.

"Oh, a guest? I'll go check."

"Don't worry about it, I'll go see who it is."

"Aw, Ma-kun! You're so nice."

"Uh, I'm not trying to be."

But he didn't feel like admitting that if he didn't take the initiative here, he'd lose his chance to do anything at all.

But when Masato stepped into the entrance hall, he found it full of people.

"Um… What's going on…?"

Pocchi and the other roustabouts were all here, along with a bunch of middle-aged women carrying what looked like boxes of cookies. There were so many of them they couldn't all fit inside, and the line stretched out the front door.

The second Masato appeared, one woman grabbed Pocchi, hauled him forward, and they both bowed.

"Oh, there you are! I just wanted to apologize for all the trouble my boy caused!"

"Uh, um… Yesterday was my bad."

"Pocchi! You're seventeen and you still can't apologize properly! Try again!"

"O-okay! I'm really sorry for the trouble I've caused you!"

The fact that this middle-aged-looking dude with a Mohawk was only two years older than Masato was certainly a terrifying discovery, but moving right along.

He recognized this woman's plump figure and face—she was the woman from the general store. Apparently, this was Pocchi's mom. Pocchi's mom bowed her head again and again, extremely apologetic.

So was everyone else. "Sorry about my boy!" "My fool of a son caused you so much grief!" The other mothers and sons began apologizing in kind, their words of atonement echoing through the run-down inn until the reverb seemed ready to knock the place down entirely.

They were clearly intent on apologizing for the rampage from the day before.

Um, so…

"M-Mooom! Help! Heeeelp meeee!"

Masato was simply not equipped to handle this, so he called the one who was.

The inn remained far too run-down to actually invite anyone in.

So they set up seats in the yard, served up tea, calmed everyone down, and talked.

That is, since Masato and the other kids had no idea how to handle this situation, they waited at the back, holding the boxes of cookies the mothers had given them. Shiraaase waited with them.

Mamako was on the front lines, receiving apologies.

"...You don't say? Well, thank you for coming all this way."

"No, no, not at all. I really can't apologize enough."

Pocchi's mother had come forward again as the representative of the Mother-Son Apology Brigade. "Hey! You say it, too!" "R-right! I'm sorry!" When prompted, Pocchi joined in.

"What my son did is not easily forgiven... I can't believe he would do this to someone's house."

"Oh, well, a lot of this was already pretty broken, so it isn't that bad, really..."

"But it is! This is just unforgivable. I work at the general store, and we handle building materials, so you simply must allow us to repair everything! Please let us help! I'm begging you!"

Well, good.

At the back, Masato and the others started whispering. "So our guild base is gonna get fixed up." "Seems like it. Sweet." "That's a windfall for sure." "A what?" "A surprising bit of luck." Not literally the wind falling. Anyway.

Back on the front lines:

"Then leave fixing this building up to us! We'll get it done in no time!"

"W-well... It seems rude to refuse, so I suppose I must accept. Thank you so very much."

"Not at all! We're the ones who should be thanking you! ...Oh, but this won't even begin to make up for it... I know! Mamako!"

"Yes? What is it?"

"You're all adventurers, right? Are you here to climb the tower?"

"Yes, we are. That was the plan...but then we heard that the children in town had all gone into the tower and never came home, and that's how we knew we had to go—"

"Oh my! You're trying to bring them back?"

"Yes. We hoped we could do something. So that's why we made this guild. It's called Mom's Guild, and—"

"My, my! Goodness gracious! You made a guild! Then we simply must help you! There are so many children who still haven't come home, so we must help in any way we can! Don't you agree?"

Pocchi's mother turned to the crowd, who all nodded vigorously. Masato wondered exactly what sort of help she was offering…

…when Pocchi and his roustabouts turned toward Masato's party. They all started yelling, "Leave it to us!" or "We'll help!" with lots of confidence.

Did they mean…? Really?

Masato and the others started whispering again. "Looks like we're solving not only the base repairs but our personnel shortage." "We are so lucky." "This is a godsend." "A god…what?" "A coincidence that works in out favor." Basically the same thing as a windfall. Anyway.

The moment finally came. They would certainly offer to have their children join the guild. What a delightful thing that would be! They would finally have enough people to tackle this tower. Here it came! Here it came!

Pocchi's mother said it!

"In that case, Mamako, let us mothers join your guild! All us mothers together can tackle that tower, no problem!"

Anyway.

Outside the ruined inn stood Masato's party all geared up. Shiraaase, too.

And with them was a line of thirteen mothers all dressed up for going out, carrying large bags stuffed with lord knows what.

Eighteen people in all. These were the Mom's Guild members! Let's conquer this tower!

No, wait.

"Mm? What's happening? I feel like I'm seeing things… Oh, I get it. Somebody must've cast an illusion spell on me—"

"Masato. I know how you feel, but what you are seeing is the truth."

"Don't you dare avert your eyes… Not that I believe my eyes, either."

"I—I can hardly believe it myself, but it's the truth!"

"For real…?"

Yes. As the grim countenances of his party proclaimed, it was all true.

Pocchi's mother as well as the hoodlums' thirteen mothers were, beyond all doubt, members of Mom's Guild. Not even joking, they had actually joined.

Masato was so lost. He really needed someone to explain.

"Um, Shiraaase... Do you mind?"

"Yes? What is it?"

"The town's mothers have become guild members. People who should never be in guilds are now in a guild. You yourself said that only test players or adventurer NPCs could join guilds. I distinctly remember you saying that at breakfast."

"I did say exactly that. But I didn't get to finish my sentence."

"And the rest was...?"

"'But this time, all town NPCs will be allowed to join.'"

"Why would you ever do something like that?"

"I thought it was a great way to secure the numbers Mom's Guild needs. This is not a lack of basic humanity on my part at all. But it seems I was entirely right about your reaction to it being extremely entertaining. Heh-heh-heh."

"Argh... You've really got it in for me... That's the most visible enjoyment I've ever seen you express..."

"And so, please take on the tower with this crowd of mothers. I will spend the day pursuing infooormation related to the Libere Rebellion once more. Farewell!"

She patted Masato on the shoulder, laughed in his face again, and went away.

She was then replaced by Pocchi and the roustabouts.

"Hey, Masato, you look kinda bothered."

"Damn straight! ...If your group would've just joined the guild instead, this would never have happened..."

"Uh... Yeah, but... About that... The guild name is just..."

The guild Mamako had created was named Mom's Guild, a name men everywhere refused to even utter aloud. "It's just..." "Yeah..." It was just too much for Pocchi's group to handle. Masato could hardly blame them.

"So anyway! We won't join the guild, but we'll fix your base up for you! Have fun storming the tower! Bye!"

"Ah! Wai—!"

Pocchi's goons quickly shuffled away.

And with that, reality took hold. Knowing when to give up was vital. There was no stopping the situation now.

"Let's go conquer a tower! Come on, everyone!"

""""""Yeah!""""""

At Mamako's call, Mom's Guild set out.

Pocchi and his gang saw them off from the ruined inn's entrance. The confidence they'd all shown earlier was clearly directed at base repairs.

Wait, no! Bodies and skills honed on the front lines of combat belonged here! It's not too late, you fools! Join us at the tower! Masato wanted to yell.

But Mamako spoke to him first.

"Ma-kun, please understand. If they join the tower assault, that rebellion might show up. And the town mothers don't ever want their children getting mixed up with them again. You see?"

"Argh, I get it! I know I have to understand how parents worry! I know I can't just ignore those concerns! I get it, okay?"

"My! You've finally learned to understand how Mommy feels? Mommy is so happy to see how you've matured, Ma-kun!"

"So glad to hear it! Ugh…"

Masato wondered if part of being mature meant forcing yourself to agree to disagreeable things.

And they were off. Mom's Guild moved down the hill, headed for the tower.

Masato and Mamako were at the lead, with Wise, Medhi, and Porta right behind.

And behind them: the mob of moms.

"Such beautiful weather."

"Yes, indeed. It really is a lovely day. I hung the futons out!"

"Oh, you did, too? So did I! And I left all the windows wide-open to air the house out."

"By the way, that side dish you gave me the other day was so delicious! I'll have to repay you soon."

"Oh, don't worry about it. I made too much! I was happy you took it off my hands. There's more where that came from, too!"

"Don't mind if I do! Saves me the trouble of making one myself. Hee-hee."

The thirteen mothers followed along, chattering away like they would on any street corner.

A Normal Hero. A Sage. A Cleric. A Traveling Merchant.

And behind them, the Normal Hero's Mother, who'd somehow joined in the gossip, and then a mom, a mom, a mom, a mom, a mom, a mom, a mom, a mom, a mom, and...

What was even going on here?

This is so stupid... What will people think of this...?

There was only one answer.

"...What are they thinking? Are they planning on clearing the tower with *them*? Are they nuts?!"

Amante was watching Mom's Guild's march from behind a tree. Her opinion was certainly the right one: No one with any sense would choose to assemble this party. Attempting to clear a tower with a pack of moms was beyond foolhardy—it was downright *mad*.

But even so...this expedition was led by Mamako Oosuki.

"There's no way this makes sense, but Mamako Oosuki is definitely on her way up the tower. We can't afford to let our guards down. We can't just let this happen. We need to prepare countermeasures... Oh, I know! I have the perfect item."

Amante took a small crystal out of her pouch, grinning.

"We still have plenty of crystal bombs back at the tower... If we place them properly and detonate them just as they head in... Mwa-ha-ha! Go on, go! We'll be ready for you! Heh-heh-heh... Bwa-ha-ha-ha!"

And with that loud peal of laughter, Amante set her scheme in motion.

Mamako marched the mob of moms down the hill and into town.

As they headed down the main road, everyone stopped to stare. Masato hunched over, keeping his head down, but somehow he survived the trial.

They headed out onto the bridge to the island. Almost at the tower entrance now.

"*Sigh...* Just getting this far has already done a number on my mental health..."

"Ma-kun! Cheer up! We're just getting started!"

"Yeah, you're right. We can finally start clearing this tower. It's the adventure we've been waiting for... Okay! Time to get myself fired up!"

They were about to begin! The entrance doors were right in front of them!

Masato was about to run forward and claim first place...when Wise beat him to it.

"Heh-heh! I'm first!"

"Argh, Wise! Let me have this one thing! ...What? Medhi and Porta, too?"

"Masato, hurry up!"

"Race you to it, Masato!"

"You're on! Let's do this!"

Masato dashed forward, making it look like he was going to catch up with the girls and pass them.

But the way Porta was running was so adorable he just wanted to run up behind her and scoop her up in his arms, but...

"*Gasp!* I can feel Mom watching!" With her keeping an eye on him, he'd better not. No, no, even without his mother's watchful eyes he never really intended to. It was just a joke.

At last, they reached the doors: Masato in the lead, Porta just behind, Medhi in third.

"Wise, you're in the rear! Loser!"

"Hey, Masato! Just how is my rear a loser?"

"Huh? No, that's an expression for 'last'..."

"I have to admit Wise's rear end is definitely not winning any competitions. I think the expression fits!"

"There's nothing wrong with my butt!"

Wise hastily clamped both hands on her backside, but she was inarguably in last place. So much for the race she'd started.

Once again, they'd got themselves all excited, and at last they were ready to start clearing this tower.

"Once we're all gathered in front of the doors, the magic circles will appear under our feet, they'll count how many we have, and then the doors will open, right?"

"I think that's how it worked. Come on, let's get this started!"

"Yeah, first we all need to gather... Huh?"

"What's going on? Mama and the mamas haven't arrived!"

"Huh? They haven't?"

They turned around, looking back. Mamako and the marching mob of moms were still on the bridge. They'd stopped in their tracks and were deep in conversation.

"Geez, what are they doing? ...I'll go check."

Masato ran back to Mamako.

"Hey, Mom, what's the holdup?"

"Oh, Ma-kun... Well, you see... This lady here..."

Mamako pointed to a mother. She was staring at the ground, white as a sheet.

Was she suddenly scared of the task ahead? She was just a villager. Normally she'd never come to a dungeon. It was only natural to be frightened. Perhaps that's how things should be.

Masato took a breath to calm himself down and then asked, "...Um, are you okay?"

"Y-yeah... I... I'm just so worried..."

"I see... I suppose anyone would be worried their first time in a dungeon..."

"No, it isn't that. It's just... I left all the windows in my house open."

"Right, you left the windows... Wait, what?"

"It was such a nice day, so I wanted to air the place out... But when I was talking to the other mothers, I started to worry. My neighborhood is safe, but an area nearby has had a number of break-ins while the owners were away, and... Oh, I'm so worried! I can't seem to help it! I'd better go home and lock up."

"Uh... Th-that makes sense..."

This certainly wasn't what Masato had expected.

But...

"But you've come all this way... And to make us all stop and wait for you is...less than ideal. I don't suppose you can just leave it be...?"

But when Masato responded honestly…

"Sorry? What did you just say?"

…the mother in question opened her eyes wide, staring right at him.

Huh? What did this child say? I must be hearing things. You did not just say that. I am seriously worried here. What if something happened? If something did, would you step up? Would you compensate me for the damages?

All that was conveyed in a single wordless stare. It was terrifying.

He'd stepped in it again. This was a battle he could not win. Masato quickly changed his approach.

"Oh, right! You've definitely got to do something! What was I thinking? Ah-ha-ha!"

He had no choice. There was no arguing with her. A mother defending her home was far too dangerous an opponent.

So they needed to solve this problem quick… Aha.

"Yo, Wise! Got a sec? Over here!"

"Mm? What?"

Wise came running over. Time to put the Sage to work.

"Wise, the lady here would like to go home and shut all her windows. I was hoping your teleport magic could help take care of that quickly. Once she's done, you can bring her back here. Would that work?"

"Sure, that's easy enough."

"I live right near the general store! Do you mind?"

"As long as the person I'm teleporting knows where we're going, I can go anywhere. Let's do this!"

The tome appeared in Wise's hand. She started to chant…

…and the crowd of mothers began flocking around her.

"Oh, you can just go right home with magic? Then might I ask a favor as well?"

"Huh? …Well, okay, there's a limit to how many people I can teleport at once, but one more person shouldn't be a problem…"

"Then can I join, too? After hearing what she said, I got worried myself… Do you mind?"

"Um… W-well, going to two places won't be—"

"Then I'd like to join, too! The perfect opportunity!"

"Uh…"

Following that: "Me too!" "May I?" "If you're going there..." "If it's not too much trouble..." The crowd just kept growing.

In the end, all thirteen mothers wanted to stop by their homes.

Wise just gaped at them. A cold sweat ran down her brow.

"So, uh... Just how many teleport spells is that? ...Do I have enough MP? ...Ah-ha-haaa..."

"Good for you, Wise! You finally get a chance to shine! You can actually use all your MP!"

"Y-yeah... That is technically true... Not really what I had in mind, though..."

Yep. Masato was entirely sympathetic to that. Still.

He put his hand on her shoulder. "Wise," he said gently. "This is our adventure. Our destiny. We can't fight it."

"Argh! Your mom causes you more trouble than anyone, so this is extra convincing!"

This world revolved around mothers.

They could not clear the tower until all the mothers' concerns were alleviated.

Meanwhile, inside the tower, on the first floor—

"...Still no sign of them."

—Amante was standing with a trigger crystal in her hand, ready to detonate the explosives at any moment.

Mamako's party should have definitely arrived by now.

"...This is taking forever!"

Not a trace. None. No matter how long she waited, nobody showed up.

"Geez, what are they doing? The moment they step inside I'm gonna blow all the bombs on the floor above and bury them in rubble! ...Where *are* they? ...Maybe I should go check outside..."

Sick of waiting, Amante stepped out of the shadows, heading for the entrance.

She stood before the firmly closed doors.

"The way this works, it only checks the numbers coming in, but you can totally step outside alone," she muttered to no one in particular. Then she reached up and gave the door a push...

...with the hand holding the trigger crystal.

Instantly, there was an earsplitting noise from above her.

"Huh? What's that noise? It sounds like a baby crying... No, that's gotta be the bomb countdown starting... Uh... WHAAAA?! Th-th-th-the trigger!! I accidentally p-pressed it!! Auuuuuuughhhhh hhhhhhh!!"

Too late.

A moment later, the crystal bombs she'd placed on every floor from the second to the nineteenth all detonated at once. "Noooooooooooooo!!" A mountain of rubble collapsed to the ground.

The evil had been vanquished.

From outside the massive, sturdy tower, there was no way to tell what was happening within.

After some time, the mothers' quick flits back home were finally done.

"Thank goodness! I got all the windows shut! Now I can relax."

"I was definitely right to go back home. I had forgotten to lock the front door! What a shock. I'll lose my own head next!"

"And I'd left the kitchen window open... Oh, right, right, the community notice had shown up, so I had her use magic to pass it on to the next household. Teleportation spells are so useful!"

"They really are. I also had a package to deliver, so I had her help with that! Such a sweet girl."

"Oh, you did, too? I did the same thing! My husband and grandfather both forgot their lunches, so we made a quick extra trip. Such a help."

The regrouped mothers were already in full-on gossip mode and getting quite carried away.

Meanwhile:

"Uh, Wise? You alive?"

"...Not just to their homes, but other places, too...and then another... Ugh... No more... I'm never teleporting again... All outta MP... I'm done..."

"Wise! I've got an MP Potion! Here!"

"P-Porta... Thanks, but...I've already chugged, like, a dozen of them... I really can't take any more..."

Wise's new role as a transportation system had proven far too popular, and she was now collapsed in a heap on the bridge. Totally wiped. Unable to move. Not even enough energy to wipe the tears and other fluids away.

But they didn't have time to let her recover. They had everyone here, and it was time to go.

"Wise. I know you're tired, but it's time to go. Up and at 'em."

"Noooo... Pleeeease, have mercyyyyy... For real, though, I caaan't... I can't take a single steppp..."

"In that case, we've got no choice. We'll just have to leave you here... No, you'd be blocking traffic. We'll just have to let the ocean take you."

"Medhiii... *Sigh*... Whatever..."

"Wow! She doesn't even have the energy to protest! This is bad!"

"All right, all right... New plan."

Masato turned his back to Wise, kneeling down. "I'll carry you, so hop on." "Ughhh... This again... I'm so sorry..." When had he done this before? Wise managed to scramble up onto his back like a feeble old lady, and the piggyback was complete.

"Oof... You're heavier than I thought..."

"I don't even care if I'm heavy... *Siiigh*... This is the life..."

"You're too young to be talking like that! ...Also, like, don't you have any concerns about this?"

"Huh? Like what?"

"Never mind. If you're good, then so am I."

It really wasn't a big deal at all.

I mean, what was pressing against his back were hardly worth any "Eek! Pervert!" style shenanigans. He could barely feel them!

So whatever.

I feel like she'd definitely have made a big deal out of this when I first met her, though...

Had she changed? Or did she just no longer view Masato as a man? That bugged him.

But by giving her a piggyback ride, Masato had solved one problem. Onward!

"Okay! Let's go clear this! Come on, everyone!"

""""""Okay!""""""

Mamako let Mom's Guild forward. The gossiping continued, but this was progress at last. They set off across the bridge toward the doors.

Everyone reached the front of the tower safely. With all the delays, this felt like a minor miracle.

"But, uh... Oh, there it goes."

Magic circles appeared under their feet, and they began counting them.

Last time, they'd passed with six—Masato's party and Shiraaase. This time, they should easily make the cut, and the door would open...

...but when it did, and they saw the first floor, everyone fell silent.

"Wh-what happened? The interior has collapsed!"

What had previously been a large corridor was now a pile of rubble. A disaster area.

Like several floors above had all collapsed. You could see quite high up.

"How could this...? What happened?"

"Good question... I wonder..."

Something had clearly gone wrong, but what that was, they had no way of knowing.

Then Medhi spoke up.

"Um... Does this mean we can climb the rubble and start on a higher floor?"

"Huh? Climb the—?"

Masato looked around again, and...the fallen rubble did form a sort of staircase.

"Looks like we can! ...All right, let's give it a shot!"

"Wait, Ma-kun! Climbing on rubble might not be safe. Perhaps if it was just us, but with the town's mothers..."

"I don't think we need to worry about that. Look!"

Climbing the rubble staircase did not seem terribly difficult. His proof?

"I'll use my eyes and guide us up safely! Leave this to me!"

Porta was bounding up the rubble, leading them on a safe path. If a twelve-year-old girl could get up that easily, the mom mob should be able to handle it, too.

"Hee-hee... The Porta seal of approval!"

"Mm-hmm. Cuteness proves safety... C'mon!"

"That's right. Let's go!"

"Yeah, onward and upward! Go, go, Masatooo! Climb! Climb!"

"Wise... You seem much better now."

The more commotion she made, the more he wanted to just drop her, but he decided to let her have this one.

The guild members proceeded without traps, monsters, tedious searches for the stairs, or any of the other impediments that should have been in their way.

A while after Mom's Guild started climbing the rubble stairs...

...the rubble near the entrance shifted slightly, then started to quiver, and finally was flung aside.

Amante crawled out from under it.

"Cough...cough... Ugh, I thought I was gonna die..."

She was in one piece. Evil had not been vanquished. Evil was resilient. Stupidity had given her the resilience needed to prevail.

After checking herself for injuries, Amante stood up and looked around—around and up...

...and saw the tail end of the mom march far above. A group of moms all dressed up to clear a dungeon.

"Ah! When did they get here?!"

Her targets were already inside and had climbed all that way without even noticing her. Lord. What a blunder. What a humiliation.

"Hngggg... I've gotta hurry after them... Oh, I know! There was a warp floor around here somewhere... I can use that as a shortcut to the twenty-first floor..."

And then what? Lay an ambush?

"I need a plan... That's it! There are special traps on the twenty-first floor! If those traps are activated, lightning shoots into the windows in the exterior walls! Mwa-ha-ha! I'll make that work for me!"

With this brilliant idea, Amante laughed wildly and ran off.

This time, Mamako Oosuki and her minions were truly doomed!

Masato's party had easily reached the twentieth floor.

But it would never do to let their guard down. There was a stratum boss on every tenth floor.

They gathered before the doors, the countdown started, and the doors swung open...

"Arf, arf! Grrrrr!"

A snarling dog appeared! A boss dog! A boss doggo! Like the tenth-floor boss, clearly intentionally designed for cuteness factor but slightly bigger and stronger!

But, uh, it was still a doggy.

"Now, Ma-kun, try not to be too mean, okay?"

"We'll all be watching. Don't hurt it too much!"

"That's right, Masato! All the mothers in town are watching, and Porta has her innocent gaze on you, too."

"Masato! Um, um... Please be nice to it!"

"R-right... I'll do my best. Here goes... *Hah!*" *Thwack.*

"Heeeee?! ...Ruff..." Thud.

Masato struck the boss doggo's side with his sword.

OVERKILL! The boss doggo was defeated!

All the women were glaring at him. "And it was such a cute doggy, too... Wasn't it?" "It did seem to be a monster, though... Right?" "But even if it was... Right?" "Argh..." The mothers' whispers stung. Masato took more damage after combat than during it. All friendly fire. Whyyy?

But either way, they'd defeated the boss.

"Right! Onward! Come on, Masato! Forward maaarch!"

"I know, I know... How long am I gonna have to carry you, Wise? Geez."

Still grumbling, he started moving toward the stairs behind the doors.

At the top of those stairs was the twenty-first level. The stone floors and walls were just like what had come before, but...

"Weird... Seems pretty bright for the middle of a stone tower."

"Yeah. I wonder... Oh, there's your answer. See? There's big holes in the walls. Like windows. Light from outside's coming in through those."

"Oh, I see."

Wise was pointing over his shoulder, and when Masato looked that way, he did in fact see huge gaps in the walls. Peering through, he saw a hole in the next wall over, too.

And through the hole in the wall beyond that, he could see the sky. That must be the tower's exterior wall. Light was pouring in through that gap.

"These let such a nice breeze in! ...Okay, Ma-kun! Here's where the real conquest begins. Let's all be on our guard!"

"Yeah... Whoa, monsters alrea—?"

"Hyah!"

Before Masato could even finish warning the others, Mamako swatted them away. Normal combat was as it had always been and would always be. Mom's Guild pressed on...

...until just then:

"Um, may I say something?" asked a member of the mom mob quietly.

"Yeah? What is it?"

"It's just... Do you mind if we take a quick look outside?"

"Outside? What for...?"

Through this hole, then the next, then the next—she wanted to go all that way and take a look outside?

Come to think of it, it did seem darker out there.

"Huh, looks like it's getting overcast..."

"Right? So you see, I'm just a little worried."

"Worried...?"

"Yes, I mean, it was such a lovely morning, right? So I hung out the laundry to dry. So..."

"That's right! If it started raining, it would be a disaster! I've got all the futons hanging out to dry! If they got wet..."

"The laundry might be fine, but futons would be a different story..."

"Oh, but the laundry would be bad enough! You'd have to wash everything again tomorrow! That would take so much time, and where would you hang it? What a mess."

"Yes... This could be bad... We'll have to do something..."

Now all the moms were gathered around, and every last one of them was fretting.

Hmm... But...

"But I mean...laundry and futons? Not really a big deal... Besides, it might not even rain... And we've come this far, so..."

Masato just wanted to keep pressing on.

""""Excuse me? What did you just say?"""""

This terror again: a crowd of moms fixing him with their fiercest glares!

Laundry and futons aren't a big deal? What are you even saying? Of course they're a big deal! Have you even done laundry before? Do you know the kind of hard work that goes into it? And on a daily basis? Are you saying that with full knowledge of the facts? And if not, how dare you say anything at all! Right? Right? Right? Right? Right?

Their terrifying gazes seemed to say as much as they loomed over him.

The cold sweat was flowing freely now. Masato quickly switched tactics! Manners!

"G-good point! Laundry and futons are everything! Our first priority! Ah-ha-ha! What was I thinking? We'd better head right back! ...Which means... Wise, you're up!"

The moment Masato said her name, every mother's eyes turned to Wise. Nobody said what they wanted her to do, but clearly, they all expected her magic to save the day again.

Wise let out a squeal, her eyes widening.

"Wha—?! W-w-wait... I...I dunno if I... Oh, y-yeah! I'm afraid I'm totally out of MP, so I can't use teleportation magic!"

"Don't worry, Wise! I still have lots of MP Potions!"

"POOOOOORTAAAAAA! SHUT UUUUUUUUUP!"

"Mmphhmffmff?!"

Wise gracefully bounded off Masato's back, hopped onto Porta in a flash, and clamped a hand over her mouth, hard. She wouldn't allow her to say another word.

But given how nimbly she'd just moved, Wise had clearly made a full recovery.

"Yo, Wise. I know how you feel, but this is a real problem... If we try to fight it, it'll be way worse, so...we're counting on you here."

"Wise, dear... If you really can't, we understand, but... There isn't much else we can do, see?"

"Whatever, Masato. Mamako, I get that, but I just... I can't..."

"Wise, fortitude! Chug another dozen MP Potions! Make your belly swell!" *Snort.*

"Medhiiiiiii! Like this doesn't involve... Oh, I know! You can ask Medhi! Medhi can use teleport magic, too!"

The moment these words left Wise's lips, Medhi went pale. All the blood had drained from her face.

"Wh-whaaat?! Um... Wait... Wise? How did you know I could...?! I've never said a word about it!"

"Huh? Oh yeah. I never asked you."

"Huh? ...Huh?!"

Both Wise and Medhi looked equally surprised.

So.

"I was just lashing out, but...you can actually use teleport magic, then?"

"Um... W-well..."

"You can, right? You totally can. And you kept quiet about it, didn't you? And you didn't even try to help at all, right? There I was, on the brink of death, and you just stood there watching, not lifting a finger to help, did you not? You did, didn't you?! I knew it!"

"Um, um... Well, I, uh... Heh-heh... I dunno!"

Faced with Wise's relentless glare, Medhi the diabolical plastered a beautiful smile on her face and tried to worm her way out of it, to no avail.

Everyone was staring at her. A silent, relentless stare.

She would have to give.

Large tears welling up in the corners of her eyes, Medhi produced the biggest smile of her life.

"Porta! Bring me two dozen MP Potions, if you have that many! If you don't, that's fine, too! You don't even need to tell me you have any!"

"No, I do! I have plenty of stock, so leave it to me!"

"Heh-heh, you're so dependable, Porta! Well done!"

Medhi had far less MP than a Sage like Wise. Her brutal struggle had only just begun.

Using the Exit Key Porta had obtained, they briefly stepped outside, and another Return Home Festival began. Weeping, Medhi knocked back MP Potions, her belly visibly swelling.

Meanwhile...

...Amante appeared on the twenty-first floor.

"Th-this makes no sense... They should be here by now..."

Tired of waiting, Amante began prowling the floor, peering into the holes in the walls. No signs of anyone.

"What's going on? ...They didn't jump to a higher floor, did they? ...Huh?!"

Amante suddenly felt a presence.

She quickly turned around and saw a giant lizard. Well, not *that* giant; it wasn't exactly a threat, but it was a monster nonetheless.

"Phew... I thought I'd finally found them, and it was just a monster! ...Ugh! Well, guess I'll just have to take care of this one!"

Amante pulled her thin sword and prepared to blow off some steam...and a moment later...

...a bolt of lightning shot out of the clouds outside. It entered through the holes in the exterior walls and struck Amante's sword, electrifying it. "BWACCCK!" She let out a strange noise.

Naturally, her hair stood up on end. Every last folicle was fried.

"R-right... If you use metal weapons on this floor, there's a set chance lightning will strike...with a stun effect so you can't move... and the static...gives you an Afro..."

Just as she spoke, Amante fell over, unable to move.

The giant lizard crept up on her. A bunch of little lizards gathered around it.

"Wow, Mom! So much food!"

"Yes, indeed. It was just lunchtime, too! Let's take her to our lair and eat her up!"

""""Yaaay!""""

It was unclear if this conversation actually took place, but either way, Amante was dragged slowly away.

Once again, the evil had been vanquished.

It was now just after noon. Mom's Guild was taking a break.

Since they were outside anyway, they'd figured they should eat. They spread out blankets around the tower entrance and were enjoying a picnic.

"Hmm? I just noticed, but it's only cloudy around the tower."

"Oh, you're right! Maybe we needn't have worried. I suppose we could have left the laundry hanging outside after all…"

"Yes… But oh well. Ours was already dry, so let's call it good."

"Yes, let's. Would you like a second helping? I stopped by a takeout shop while I was back home and bought a bunch. There's plenty where that came from!"

"I also stopped by a shop and bought some sides. Help yourself!"

"Don't mind if I do… Oh, that is good! I'll have to buy some on my way home."

"Yes. I'm thinking this should be tonight's dinner."

The mob of moms were, as usual, chattering away while they ate.

Meanwhile, there was one person at death's door.

"*Sniff…* I drank too many MP Potions… Oh, my aching belly… I'm done for… I'm a failure as a woman… My heart's been torn to shreds…"

"What shreds? You're all jiggly! See?" *Jiggle.*

"Wise! Don't poke— U-urp…"

It seemed she would live. Medhi was merely experiencing the death of her femininity. Her clothing had been unable to contain the swelling, and she was lying on her back, her belly exposed—truly, a fate no girl could endure.

Especially with a boy around.

It is just her belly... But still... I do wish they'd be more mindful of my presence...

Masato wasn't exactly against having beautiful bellies on display, but a part of him was definitely against this entire situation.

That aside.

Masato decided to reassess the situation. Some serious thought was in order.

"Right, everyone, listen up. I've got a question here. Despite doing a real number on both Wise and Medhi, we've barely made any actual progress on the tower... Anyone have any ideas?"

Masato looked around at the girls sharing his blanket. He wasn't even trying to hide his frustration.

No one seemed inclined to speak first.

"Ideas? ...I mean, sure, I have some thoughts, but..."

"They're definitely holding us back in a lot of... Urp... If I talk, it almost comes up..."

"Oh, uh... Medhi, you're good. Just take it easy for now."

"Um, um... I...think we should just try harder! I think that...might help... Ohh..."

"Don't worry, Porta. I know what you mean."

The reason for their lack of progress was clear. They had a group with them that insisted on slowing the party down. Everyone knew it, and they were right here, so no one wanted to say so aloud.

And even knowing the problem, figuring out how to deal with it was easier said than done.

They needed the numbers, so they couldn't just send them home. The only way to progress smoothly was with their cooperation... but they had their own thoughts on things, and attempting to ignore those feelings led to terrifying glares.

"*Sigh...* I knew this was gonna be rough from the start, but...I didn't think it would be *this* bad..."

"I definitely thought we'd do a little better than this, too... Maybe they just don't, like, grasp the urgency?"

"Urgency... Right, that does seem to be the case. The mothers helping us are the ones who already got their kids back, after all..."

"And since their kids are back, they must be super relieved!"

"Yeah, that could be... Then again, I can't say I feel much urgency myself. This is just a game event, and if we're gonna join in, we might as well try to clear it... That's about it. But these mothers..."

Regardless of the game's difficulty... No, perhaps this *was* the main challenge provided by this particular game. Either way, dealing with mothers remained the main source of agony for the children. It was really tough sometimes...

"Ma-kun, don't worry," Mamako said. She'd been listening in silence all this time.

"But, Mom... I *do* worry..."

"Everything will be all right. Moms always come through in a pinch. No need to worry."

"...Just take your word for it?"

"That's right. You can trust your mother and trust these mothers. I promise."

Mamako's smile stretched across her entire face. It was the sort of smile that allowed no doubt, one that would reassure any son.

If Mamako said so, maybe he should believe her. Masato glanced at his companions, and Wise, Medhi, and Porta all nodded back at him.

Everyone had decided to trust her.

"...Okay. We'll trust Mom and the mothers."

With these trusted companions, they would finally start clearing this town—

"Um, pardon me."

Another interruption. One of the mothers had spoken up. When Masato turned to answer, she said, "Oh, sorry, I was speaking to Mamako." "Oh, you were?" Mamako and the mother began whispering together.

They were looking at a piece of paper—maybe a flyer of some sort.

Mamako suddenly turned around and looked at Masato.

"Hee-hee! Ma-kun! This is Mommy's moment!"

She seemed even more upbeat than usual. Her smile shone even brighter than before. A Mother's Light was at full power, and her entire frame was glowing.

Now Masato felt nothing but worry.

*   *   *

Meanwhile, inside the tower—

—the evil was resurrected a second time.

"Geez. As if I'd let myself get eaten by a bunch of chump monsters."

Amante shot an angry glance over her shoulder, and the giant lizard family turned and fled… They were too low level to bother killing.

So.

"*Sigh*… Getting hit by the trap I set for them… How pathetic… Next time… No, that's not right."

Amante began walking, carefully fixing her hair.

"It was a mistake to even rely on traps. Clearly. I should handle this myself. And wandering around looking for them is a mistake, too. I know they're coming. I just have to wait somewhere I know they'll have to come. Right."

Muttering to herself, Amante proceeded with confidence across the floor and up the stairs. On the floor above, she either glared or kicked the monsters away, advancing even higher.

Then she reached the stairs to the thirtieth floor.

"Yes, here. If I wait here, they're sure to come. All I have to do is wait. Yes."

Amante sat down on the stairs. Waiting. Patiently.

"Yes, hurry up and come to me! I, Amante, will personally take you down! Mwa-ha-ha."

Amante continued to wait.

She would stay that way until her enemy appeared. For as long as it took. For ages.

Meanwhile, Masato's party…

…was at the harbor.

"Step right up! Time for our monthly deep discount! Freshly caught fish, shellfish, shrimp, and crab! Stuff your baskets full for three thousand mum! Buy everything you need for tonight's dinner! Come one, come all!"

A fisherman stood near mountains of seafood, bellowing for attention.

The mob of moms attacked!

"The monthly feast! We can't let it get away!"

"As long as it stays in the basket during checkout, you're gold! Pile as much as you can fit!"

"Oh, I will! I'll make such a pile! Hahhhh! Clams, clams, shrimp, fish, fish, fiiish!!"

"Amateurs! The trick is to use the shrimp and crab claws to stabilize the pile!"

"Ohhh, is that the best you can do? Heh. You haven't seen anything yet!"

The mothers were all stuffing baskets with seafood, piling them higher and higher. Their hands moved at lightning speed, like a hundred-punch combo from a master martial artist.

Flat baskets piled ten inches, twenty inches, thirty inches high.

One mother had even managed to get her seafood tower over a yard tall.

It was needless to say who—Masato himself certainly wouldn't. He never would, but…

…It was Mamako.

"Look, look, Ma-kun! Look how much I got! Mommy comes through in a pinch!"

"Uhhh, sure… Right…"

Masato, Wise, Medhi, and Porta were all overwhelmed by the mothers' grim determination. All they could do was watch.

After that, the mothers all said they had to start getting dinner ready, like this was plainly obvious. Nobody took a step toward the tower.

Masato's party retreated to their base with a mountain of seafood.

"Oh, you're back! We've been waiting! …So whaddaya think? Pretty awesome, right? We worked our butts off turning this place into a gorgeous hotel!"

Pocchi and his goons proudly showed them a magnificent building, which was now like some sort of palace: walls and pillars of beautiful marble, gorgeous gardens full of colorful flowers all around the property, and a fountain in the path leading to the entrance, decorated with a statue that looked suspiciously like Mamako.

The inn formerly on the verge of collapse had been leveled up to a luxury hotel in less than a day! It was now the Mom's Guild Hotel!

Masato couldn't help dashing over to Pocchi and gazing at him all teary-eyed.

"Th-this... This is so...so... *Sniff...!*"

"Heh-heh. Now, now, Masato. I know you're impressed, but it ain't good for a man to start bawling. But hey, I know the feelin'. Heh-heh."

"*Sniff!* No, that's not it! That isn't it! *Hnnng!*"

If only they'd had Pocchi's men with them, they'd have made it through that tower without so much as breaking a sweat. Why couldn't that power had been turned toward better things?

He so badly wanted to make that point but was too busy shedding tears of frustration to say a word.

Mom's Guild Daily Report

Occupation: Guild Master
Name: Mamako Oosuki

Business Report:

The mothers from town became guild members! We immediately set to work clearing all sorts of important mom quests, like locking up the houses, taking in the laundry, and checking out a sale on seafood. These mothers are so reliable!
Mommy wants to continue clearing quests just like this!

Other Notes:

Here is a list of the teatime snacks I brought back with me:
Roll cake from the Seaside Ma'am cake shop (1,900 mum for six inches)
Madeleine assortment from À Roux Chantier sweet shop (2,300 mum for sixteen pieces)
Dorayaki from Umigameya Japanese confectionary shop (2,200 mum for twelve pieces)
Any others I can't fit in this space will go on another page.

Member Comments:

Please try to remember what our actual goal here is. Otherwise imma cry.

The macarons were so good! I'm gonna go buy some more!

I can't taste anything but MP Potions anymore... Urp...

It'll all keep for ages in my shoulder bag! Leave storing things to me!

Chapter 4 The Courage to Accept Things. A Loving Heart. Also, Full-Body Armor. That's What a Mother Needs... Wait, Armor?

Thanks to the efforts of Pocchi and the roustabouts, Mom's Guild's base had been transformed from a ruined inn to a luxury hotel.

The change was dramatic both inside and out. Windows that had lacked both glass and frames were now super fancy and covered in elegant trimmings. The floors that had previously been more prone to breaking than providing support were now hardwood and so polished that it seemed a shame to tread on them at all. Even the halls were lavishly decorated with tasteful flower arrangements.

They were in the first-floor restaurant lounge of this high-class hotel.

"Okay, everyone... Hands together!"

""""Thanks for the food!"""""

Once again, the day started with their usual chant and a super Japanese breakfast.

The Normal Hero, the Normal Hero's Mother, the Sage, the Cleric, and the Traveling Merchant—joined once again by the Mysterious Nun. Everyone was munching away...or at least, almost everyone.

The hero Masato was staring fixedly at the fish head sticking out of his miso soup bowl, not moving a muscle.

"...Um, Mom? What the heck is this?"

"*Arajiru!* Have I never made it before?"

The *ara* referred to the head and bones left after cleaning a fish, which were then used to make a stock (or *jiru*) for miso soup. There are even regional variations that leave the miso out entirely.

This was the result of attempting to use every bit of the bounty gathered at yesterday's seafood sale. Bravo, Mamako. Housewife power! Well done.

You might think sinister miso soup with fish heads and bones floating in it would be unpopular, but nope: "This is crazy good!" "I love it." "I've never had anything like it!" "The bits of fish are so delicious!" "Watch out for the bones, though." The girls seemed to quite like it. It definitely didn't taste bad. Maybe Japanese tongues just loved anything fishy.

Moving right along.

The more excited people got about yesterday's bounty, the more annoyed Masato got.

"*Sigh*... Look, Mom, if you don't mind..."

"Oh, you want seconds?"

"That's not... Mom, I really don't think our goal yesterday was the spectacular seafood sale. Right?"

"Huh? O-oh, I suppose not. That wasn't our original goal. We were going to clear that tower, right?"

"Yeah, so—"

"So whyyyyyyy didn't you ever show up?!" screamed someone not seated at the table.

Following this scream, the window in the restaurant lounge was kicked in, and something came flying through it.

Covered in glass, the something rolled across the floor, then scrambled to its feet—it was Amante, apparently totally fine with having all those shards of glass stuck in her.

"Wh-whoa, are you okay?"

"This doesn't hurt a bit! And in any case... You bunch! What the heck?! You were supposed to attack the tower yesterday, weren't you?! I thought you were insane to put nothing but moms in your party, but even so, you set out to climb it, didn't you?! Didn't you?!"

"Uh, yeah... Exactly right. Even the part about having nothing but moms being totally insane."

"Then why didn't you ever get anywhere? You at least made it as far as the twentieth floor, but that's it! Nothing after that! Whyyy?!"

"Um... Well... They had to go home and lock up, then take in their laundry, then there was a sale, so... The mothers kept finding reasons to go back to town, so..."

"Huh?! What?! That doesn't even make sense! Are you yanking my chain?!"

"That was exactly my reaction..."

"I really shouldn't be telling you this, but you realize I thought you were coming, set a trap, and laid in wait for you? And then I accidentally set it off and self-destructed, but then I kept waiting for you after that?! All night?!"

"Oh yeah? ...Well, that's, uh..."

Frankly, "Sounds like we were better off not making progress." "Yeah." "I think so!" The girls were carrying on with their breakfast as if nothing had happened, and they did seem to have a point.

But for the person left waiting, this was undoubtedly infuriating. She was glaring ferociously at Masato.

"And then I find you enjoying a leisurely breakfast?! Are you even *trying* to clear the tower?! Are you?!"

"Uh, well, it's not that simple... I'd love to get going soon myself, but, well..."

"Then stand up and go! Why don't you?! What's stopping you?!"

Good question.

Still focused on her meal, Wise and the others explained.

"Simple matter of numbers. The moms won't be joining us till the afternoon."

"They're going to spend the morning on housework and then get together after that. That leaves us with less time to focus on clearing the tower, but..."

"But since they got all their housework done, we can focus on the tower! Wise and Medhi won't kill themselves casting teleport magic over and over!"

Yep.

"Honestly, I'm not super satisfied with that... But unless we have the numbers, there's nothing we can do. So today we'll show up in the afternoon."

Masato was definitely working hard to convince himself this was for the best.

"...What...the...heck...? You've gotta be kidding..."

Amante was shaking, her head down, her whole body quivering. This was sheer fury. She was about to unleash hellfire on them.

And guess who poured oil on that fire.

"Um, Amante, dear—"

"Hrk! Mamako Oosuki!"

The moment Mamako tried to speak, disaster was ensured.

Amante already viewed Mamako as her mortal enemy, and the moment she laid eyes on her, detonation occurred. The explosion was enormous.

"Arghhhh! ARGHHHHHHHHHH! You're a mother! Another mother! You made a fool out of me! Mothers are the cause of all my problems! No more! I've had enough!"

"U-um, Amante? Please calm down—"

"Don't you dare speak to me! You make me sick! Arghhhh!! That's it, we're settling this right here and now!"

And with that, Amante drew her sword.

"Come at me, Mamako Oosuki! Come on! Let's do this!"

"W-wait, Amante! Take a deep breath and—"

"I agree! Amante, you need to calm down!"

"I have washing up to do! I want to get these dishes clean before the food dries out and gets stuck to them!"

"Good point! Amante, Mom's got washing up to do… Wait. Mom? That's not the argument we should be making here—"

"Argh! Then go wash up! Right now!"

"That's your priority, too?!"

"Oh… N-no, don't do that! I'm through being yanked around by what moms want! …I know!" Amante thrust her sword out, pointing at Mamako, as if she'd just had a great idea. "Mamako Oosuki! If you won't fight me because you've got dishes to do, then we'll compete over that! Let's find out which of us is better at washing up!"

Yikes.

They'd moved from the restaurant lounge to the kitchen, where rows of counters and dishwashing sinks stood.

"Uh… So Mamako versus Dumbante—"

"Hey, you there, Sage! Get my name right!"

"Mamako versus In-Over-Her-Head in a dishwashing battle."

"You, Cleric! You didn't even say part of my name!"

But Wise and Medhi ignored Amante's howls and started things off.

Mamako stood before the sink to the right.

"I didn't intend to make this a fight, but I do want to get the dishes done."

Amante stood before the sink to the left.

"This *is* a fight! Even if it's washing dishes, I won't lose to any mothers!"

Two contestants: Mamako all smiles, Amante's throbbing veins about to burst.

"*Siiigh...* Why'd things have to end up this way? ...Anywho, if we don't do this, Amante's just gonna keep shouting, so go ahead. Let's find out who's best at washing up," Masato said. "Positions!"

"Start washing!" Porta yelled.

And with that, the battle began!

Each sink contained three sets of the dishes they'd used for that morning's breakfast. Whoever got them all washed first was the winner.

"Let's go! If we assigned a number to my washing power, it would be at least 530,000! Watch and weep!"

Moistening her sponge, Amante started with the teacups, then the small plates for seaweed and pickles, then the miso soup and rice bowls, and finally the platters that had contained the eggs.

Moving from the least to the most dirty was a core principle of dish-washing. Amante was surprisingly good at this.

"Heh-heh! I'm actually great at all kinds of housework! I've got the skills needed to survive without a mother! ...Well, Mamako Oosuki? Will you admit defeat?!"

Certain she'd already won, Amante glanced at the sink to her right.

Mamako was tackling her dishes without a sponge. Instead, she was holding Altura.

"Now, then! Let's get started!"

"Wha...? Mamako Oosuki?! Why are you holding a sword?!"

"So I can do *this*!"

Mamako turned all the dishes in the sink upside down, making sure they didn't overlap.

Then she poured a small amount of dish soap on the tip of her sword and held it over the dishes.

When she did, the sword began spraying water—mingled with just the right amount of soap—as if mimicking the interior workings of a dishwasher.

Once the backs of the dishes were clean, she flipped them and sprayed them again.

"Okay, all done."

"Huhhhhhhhh?!"

Mamako had already finished. "W-wait a minute!" Amante cried, peering into Mamako's sink. She picked up a dish and inspected it closely, astonished. "Not a speck on it… So much cleaner than washing it by hand…and faster. My God… Washing dishes with water from a sword…?"

"Yesterday our base didn't have running water, so I wondered if I could use this sword instead, and when I tried it out, it worked just like that! Such a help. This sword is very useful. Hee-hee!"

"Useful? …That's not even what a sword is for! That's not fair!" Amante protested.

And the decision went to the judges. Masato turned to Shiraaase to get her opinion.

"So, Shiraaase. What say you to Amante's argument?"

"Whether using a legendary sword as a dishwasher is appropriate or not, the standards for judging washing are speed and cleanliness. I believe the precise methods are up to the contestants. Just as some people use dishwashers, and others always wash by hand."

"So you believe in respecting one another's differences. I see. Thank you… So there you have it, Amante."

"B-but… Then…"

The match was over. Shiraaase's final decision:

"The winner of the dishwashing contest is…Mamako!"

"Oh my! I guess I win!"

Mamako lined her dishes up on the drying rack and was done. Meanwhile, Amante hadn't finished rinsing. Her sink was still filled with bubbles. The results were clear.

Mamako had destroyed her.

"Congrats, Mamako!"

"You win even when you aren't trying to... That's Mamako for you."

"Mama is the best at mom stuff! I have so much respect!"

"Thank you, Mamako. With this victory, you've earned the right to compete in the WMC—that's the World Mom Championship. How do you feel right now?"

"Well... As Ma-kun's mommy, I'm just glad I could avoid embarrassing him. Thanks to everyone who supported me!"

"You being in this at all is already embarrassing, so please don't mention me."

That aside, Mamako had won. Her party gathered around her, celebrating the victory.

Meanwhile, Amante the loser was genuinely upset and repeatedly pounding her fist against the floor.

"Argh... How...? I never saw it coming!"

"Oh, Amante. It was a dumb fight, but, like...you already lost, so—"

"No, this isn't over! ...This must be some mistake! ...Yes! This is all wrong! There's no way my washing power could ever be less than Mamako's!"

"Can we move off the dishwashing thing already? Like, please, just choose something else."

Masato's polite suggestion fell on deaf ears.

Amante picked herself up off the floor and glared at Mamako.

"Mamako Oosuki! I challenge you again! Fight me once more!"

"B-but... Amante, dear, let's not. You see, I need to wash Ma-kun's shirts next. I've got time this morning, so I want to do it properly."

"Yeah, Amante. Mom's busy. She's got to wash my shirts, or... Wait, if you say that she'll—"

"Then I challenge you to a shirt-washing contest! We'll see which of us washes them better!"

"I knew it... Mom, you don't have to accept—"

"I accept! Nobody can make Ma-kun's shirts whiter than me!"

"Whoa! Mom's suddenly super fired up!!"

Mamako would never lose to anyone where her beloved son was concerned. This was a matter of pride.

Once again: yikes.

*   *   *

They moved to the guild hotel roof. The view was spectacular.

"Okay, we've got another fight that'll end in tears! Mamako versus Loserante—"

"You there, Sage! I'm not crying! Also, that's not my name!"

"Mamako versus someone who should really wash her own stinky equipment before washing someone else's shirts! A laundry battle!"

"You vile Cleric... Have you no mercy?" There go the waterworks already.

But Wise and Medhi started the battle with no sympathy for Amante's sniffles.

They'd made a boxing ring out of clotheslines, and the two contestants stepped inside.

First: the champion, Mamako, happily holding one of Masato's slightly soiled shirts.

"Hee-hee. Look! All dirty because of how hard he fights! But don't worry! You can leave the laundry to Mommy!"

Then the challenger, Amante, holding another one of Masato's shirts high.

"Masato Oosuki! I'll make your filthy little shirt as white as snow! You won't believe how fast it gets clean!"

Both of them showed off Masato's laundry to everyone there.

Masato collapsed in a heap and rolled away in the throes of agony. "Uggghhh... My last shred of privacy is deeeeaad..." Most of the stains on Masato's clothing weren't incurred in the heat of battle but from his tendency to roll around like this when he got upset. Anyway.

"The scoring is simple!" Shiraaase said. "Whoever makes Masato's shirts whiter is the winner. Ready?"

"Start the laundry battle!" Porta yelled.

Amante sprang into action.

"Cower before the skills honed camping out in that tower!"

Amante opened her item storage and pulled out a large bucket.

"Why does she have something like that?"

"Have you been using that as a bath, too?!"

"Yes, I have! I used this to splash seawater on myself! Gee, sooooorry!"

Enduring Wise's and Medhi's horrified stares, she used the tap on the roof to fill the bucket.

"And I bought *this* at the general store!"

Amante pulled out a washboard and some detergent. She put plenty of detergent on the shirt's stains and then began rubbing it against the washboard. "A washboard... Just like..." "What are *you* looking at?!" The crowd seemed poised for another boob battle, but Amante ignored them, furiously washing.

Time for the announcer. Masato was still lying in a heap, but Shiraaase demanded a comment anyway.

"Masato, the enemy boss is enthusiastically washing your shirt. What do you think about that?"

"I have no idea how to feel or what expression I should have."

Masato's mind and body were as close to nothingness as possible. He had passed through many stages and was preparing to disappear entirely.

And the stains on his shirt began to vanish. Amante's laundry was progressing well.

"Heh-heh-heh! I've almost got that stain on the sleeve! I'm amazing at laundry! ...Well, Mamako Oosuki? Ready to concede defeat?"

Amante held her results aloft, turning toward her opponent.

Mamako had not even started her laundry yet. She was just cradling Masato's shirt closely to her, looking terribly sad.

"Amante dear... I do wish you'd use a more delicate touch."

"Delicate?! Pfft. This is a contest! Delicacy has no place here!"

"I don't quite mean that. I just want you to stop because Ma-kun's shirt will fray if you rub it so forcefully."

"O-oh, *that's* what you mean? ...A f-fair point... But you need to do this to get the stubborn stains out! How else can you get it clean?"

"Oh, that's easy... You just do it like this."

Mamako held up not a washboard nor a washing machine—but Altura.

She dipped the tip of the sword into the water, which then welled out of the navy-blue blade and formed a large water sphere in the air.

She put Masato's shirt inside.

"Even if you gently wash it, those stubborn stains still come right out."

She tapped the surface of the sphere as if she were hitting the START button on a washing machine.

Just as Mamako wanted, the water in the sphere began to gently churn like it was on a delicates cycle. The shirt fluttered elegantly within the sphere, and the stubborn stains on it melted away.

Amante's jaw dropped open so hard it nearly dislocated.

"Wh-what the hell is that sword?! How can it do this?!"

"It makes all a mother's desires possible. Hee-hee!"

A mother's desires gave it the effects of a detergent and fabric softener…apparently.

Before their very eyes, the shirt's stains all vanished…

The two shirts were hung on the lines in the center of the ring, one astonishingly white and one with the dirt somewhat removed but rather frayed.

Shiraaase passed judgment.

"The winner of the laundry battle is…Mamako!"

"Hee-hee! Yay!"

The results were clear: another overwhelming victory for Mamako.

Supporters gathered around the victory, celebrating.

"I knew this would happen. It's Mamako, after all. And Masato's shirts."

"No way Mamako would ever come in second where Masato's concerned."

"Mama will never lose on Masato stuff!"

"Now, Mamako. This victory has earned you a seed placement at the WMC—that's the World Masato Championships. Can you tell us how you feel?"

"No matter how many other mothers come, I won't let anyone else claim the World Ma-kun Champion title from me!"

"Oh, God, please no. The idea of moms the world over competing to be my number one is beyond incomprehensible into straight-up living hell."

Look forward to fierce mom-offs in the World Masato Champion-ship arc, coming soon...

But all joking aside...

"W-wait! ...There's no way I'd ever lose to a mom... It doesn't make sense! I haven't lost yet!"

Amante's cry cut through the celebratory mood.

"Amante... Are you still going—?"

"It's just a fact! I haven't lost! ...I—I know! This is a three-round fight! So I haven't lost yet!"

"Yeah, okay, she's an idiot."

"Even if it was a three-round fight, she's already lost two out of three, so that wouldn't change anything."

"The third battle has a hundred times the points! Whoever wins the third fight is the real victor! Settled! The last battle... Uh... It'll take place in the tower! Let's do that! We're done with laundry, right? No more laundry? Then lock your doors and let's get going! All right?"

With that unilateral declaration, Amante ran off to the fence around the roof.

"I don't owe you an explanation or anything, but since some idiots came wandering back, our forces are primed and assembled! Prepare yourselves!"

And with that, Amante jumped...

...off the hotel roof. *Whoosh— Thud!* Boy, that sure sounded painful...

They ran to the edge and looked down, and Amante seemed to be totally fine, just hopping mad. She ran off. She was clearly pretty durable!

So.

"Lock up and get going... I'd love to, but..."

They weren't meeting the other mothers until the afternoon. They couldn't get going until then. And they'd explained this to Amante, so...let's just assume explanations are wasted on the stupid.

But then...

"Masato, c'mere."

"We might be able to get going right away."

...Wise and Medhi were both staring over the edge of the roof.

At what? Well...

*　　*　　*

"Excuse me! Mamako! Everyone! Are you here?"

Responding to the call, they went to the entrance hall and found...

"...Erk..."

...them. The mob of moms.

They were all dressed up to go out, lugging overstuffed bags. Not only the moms who'd come to the tower the day before were present but a new batch of moms as well, more than double the previous number. At a glance, there looked to be around thirty of them.

As Masato stared in horror, Pocchi's mother stepped forward, extremely flustered.

"Good morning, everyone! I'm sorry to come bursting in on you like this."

"Um, uh... No, but... Why are there so many—?"

"We were talking among ourselves! We said we were trying to get back the runaway children! And then these other mothers said they wanted to help! So we gathered up all the mothers whose children ran away!"

"O-oh... Well, thanks? B-but...I thought you weren't coming until the afternoon... Don't you have housework?"

"We do! But then something came up... Look!"

Pocchi's mother showed him a small page torn out of a notebook.

Going to square things. Be right back, it read in rather nice handwriting.

"Is this...from Pocchi?"

"That's right! ...You see, yesterday, after they finished repairing your base, he came back home...and I haven't seen him since! I thought he was asleep, but when I went to his room there was no sign of him, just this note! And it said he'd be right back, but it's morning and he still isn't back!"

"So you're thinking..."

Masato stared at the note. The girls looked over his shoulder.

"Hmm... Doesn't seem like he's run away again, though."

"Yeah. I mean, he says he's coming back."

"Um... What does he mean by 'square things'?"

"That means he wants to settle the matter. Sort things out."

Shiraaase was right. It was a word often used after a fight, when someone was trying to make up for their actions.

So what was Pocchi trying to square?

The whole runaway thing? The guild attack? Either way...

It seemed safe to assume he was trying to do something about Amante, the cause of all this.

In which case...

"...They most likely went to the tower."

"You think so? That's what we thought! When I talked to the other mothers, I found out all the children who came home two days ago did the same thing! They've all disappeared!"

"All of them? ...Then they've got decent numbers. Enough to hit the requirement for the tower..."

"That's right! So! So...!"

It wasn't just Pocchi's mother; it was every mother unaware of their child's whereabouts, all with tears in their eyes, hands clasped together in prayer, eyes pleading with Masato's party.

Desperate faces of mothers whose children had not come home, staring at them.

And one of their own was a mother, too. Mamako nodded silently.

Wise, Medhi, Porta, and even Shiraaase were all staring at Masato.

They all waited for him, for the hero's words.

"Let's make sure our houses are locked up! It's time to go!"

Mm. That was a little weird. This was really the place for simplicity. Maybe he should have left out the first part.

But everyone there nodded in agreement, as if he'd made a very good point. Locking up was very important.

The full force of Mom's Guild set out to clear the tower.

"Well, everyone! Let's get going!" Mamako yelled.

And they smoothly started moving.

"Well, I think I will accompany you."

"Mm? Shiraaase, you're coming? ...What brought that on?"

"What will happen next... As an admin—no, as an individual—I would like to witness it firsthand. Do you mind?"

"Uh, no. Not at all. You're welcome to come."

The attack formation placed Masato's party at the head, Shiraaase with them, and then the mob of moms. A large squad, more than thirty people in all.

Masato's group led the march down from the plateau, through the town, and across the bridge toward the tower.

The streets were pretty quiet today. The mothers were gossiping less, the gravity of the situation reflected in their expressions. All concerned for their children's well-being, ready for the dangers the tower held.

This was a relief to the children.

"Looks like this won't be a repeat of yesterday."

"Yeah, not having to blow all my MP ferrying them to their homes and back will be just great."

"Yes... But I do have other concerns..."

"Yeah..."

All of them were only too aware of the last thing Amante had said:

I don't owe you an explanation or anything, but since some idiots came wandering back, our forces are primed and assembled! Prepare yourselves!

They would much rather not think about what she'd meant, but... just in case, they had to be prepared. Especially for how they should handle things in front of their mothers...

As they pondered this question, they realized they'd already reached the tower.

Mom's Guild assembled before the entrance, the magic circles appeared beneath their feet, counting them, and the doors slowly swung open. They were inside the tower.

Inside the entrance stood the staircase of rubble. If they climbed that, they would soon reach the nineteenth floor.

But on the floor right in front of the rubble was an arrow with a message written below it.

Use the warp floor to get up faster. Get here a sap!

Huh.

"Uh… This is Amante, right?"

"Yeah. Can't wait for us to get to her any other way."

"And she apparently doesn't know what *ASAP* is. How sad."

"So… Can we assume this isn't a trap?"

"Yeah… If she set a trap and that delayed our arrival, that would just make her even more annoyed. Even someone who doesn't know *ASAP* is an acronym would know that."

"So if it isn't a trap…we might as well use it."

They followed the arrow on the floor around the rubble staircase, taking a different path from the one Shiraaase had once led them down, to a small door at the back.

"Here?"

He opened the door carefully, just in case. Inside was a fairly large space. There was nothing else in it, just eight magic circles on the floor. Each of them had a number from two to nine written next to it, but all the circles except eight had been stabbed with something sharp and then destroyed.

And someone had kindly written To the eighty-first floor next to the eighth magic circle.

"So this is a warp floor that will take us to the eighty-first floor. Easy to understand at least… Well, here goes nothin'."

Masato stepped onto the magic circle. Light poured out around his feet, and he felt a sudden floating sensation. He closed his eyes against the light…

…and when he opened them, he was somewhere else.

"…So this is the eighty-first floor?"

The floor was covered in unidentifiable bones, and the walls were hideous and writhing, like the group was inside the monster. The first word that popped into his mind was *hell*.

As his party members warped after him, they, too, frowned.

"Oh my… What a frightening place…"

"Blegh. This is gross."

"So repulsive… So foul… Like being inside Wise!"

"More like you, Medhi. You're the one who's all nasty inside."

"Oooh... Too awful... I'm getting really scared..."

"You are? I find it rather refreshing myself!"

Let's just ignore the mystery of what was wrong with the Mysterious Nun's taste.

With their sheer numbers, it took some time, but eventually the entire mom mob had arrived. It was time to move forward.

"Then let's start clearing this— Oh."

Masato was about to take a step forward when a monster appeared from around the corner.

Several hellhounds, all with way too many faces, charged at them. *"Hyah!"* Mamako swung both her swords. *Shnk pshhhht!* Battle complete. All done.

"Even higher-floor enemies aren't a threat... Geez, Mom... Guess nothing changes. Oh well. On we go!"

Mom's Guild began marching, Masato's party at the head, the mob of moms following behind. They took up the entirety of the wide passage.

Exploring at random would get them nowhere. They needed information. With that in mind, Masato turned to Shiraaase.

"Um, Shiraaase..."

"I have no knowledge of the routes in this sector. I'm afraid I can't act as your guide."

"O-oh... I was hoping you could..."

"I apologize for failing to live up to your expectations. All I can do is infooorm you of basic infooormation. For example, about traps that can't be avoided."

"Traps we can't avoid? They exist?"

"Yes, they do... Oh, there's one now."

A trap appeared in their path.

It was a massive stone block taking up the entire passage—big enough that they couldn't just jump over. There was an armor mark carved into it.

"So... It's just a really big version of what we saw lower down?"

"Yes. So big you can't avoid it. You must step onto it. And the trap effect—"

"We'll find that out when we step on it! Here goes! ...*Hyah!*"

"Wait! Mom?!"

Mamako had gone trotting forward and stomped right onto the stone like it didn't matter.

The next moment, the elbow guard Mamako had equipped vanished.

"O-oh! Oh dear! Ma-kun! Mommy's elbow armor vanished! I wonder why."

"Why? ... Oh, wait."

Masato tried hopping on the stone himself. His elbow guard vanished, too.

He quickly pulled up his status screen and checked his stats; his DEF value was slightly lower.

"I see. That explains it."

"Yes. Floors with the armor mark lower your defense. They make armor vanish and lower your actual defense stat."

"The heck? That sucks! Especially for mages, since we don't have much defense to begin with."

"Yes... For Wise and myself this could be... Oh, but we've got Mamako, so we'll never actually fight."

"Oh, right! There's no chance of anyone attacking us. In that case..."

Wise hopped onto the armor icon. Her cape vanished.

Medhi joined her, and the sleeves of her healer tunic vanished, leaving her sleeveless.

"Wow. You both look like you're dressed for warmer weather."

"Yeah. This isn't that bad. Definitely gives me a little freedom of movement."

"It feels like I just changed clothes! It's actually sort of fun."

"Um, Ms. Shiraaase! I'm a noncombatant and have no defense, so what will happen if I step on it?"

"You'll just have to step on it and find out. I'll join you. Come on!"

Porta and Shiraaase stepped onto the tile. "Whoa!" Porta's sleeves grew shorter. "Hmm." The hem of Shiraaase's skirt grew slightly higher.

"Seems to activate regardless of whether you're a combatant or not..."

"I suppose it'll have a similar effect on all the moms... But none of them can participate in combat to begin with, so I guess we can assume there's no risk involved."

"Yeah. So...let's keep moving!"

And with that, the entire Mom's Guild began making their way over the armor tile. "Oh my!" "Goodness!" All the mothers lost portions of their best clothes, and this surprised them, but nothing more.

A while later...

"...Oh, there are the stairs!"

They'd stumbled onto the stairs fairly quickly. Masato went up first.

The eighty-second floor. It was the same sort of hellish castle as the floor below.

And once again, there was a tile with an armor mark.

"This again? ...Is there one of these on every floor?"

Were they going to have to step on these each time they reached a new floor? And the effect would keep stacking until they found a trap Rilascio tile.

Their defense dropping, their armor vanishing...

But...more and more skin showing...?

Seemed likely. After all, what they were wearing vanished.

Okay, then.

"Masato, are you enjoying this?" Shiraaase asked.

"Uh, well... Uh, oh, no, not like that!" He vehemently denied it, but...

Mom's Guild was progressing smoothly.

Each floor they reached had an armor trap floor, and they found no signs of any trap Rilascio tiles. More and more armor vanished, and more and more skin came into view.

Eighty-third floor.

"Hey! My jacket's gone!"

Eighty-fourth floor.

"Eeek! My skirt's absurdly short now!"

Eighty-fifth floor.

"Uh... My shirt vanished..."

Eighty-sixth floor.

"Whoa! I don't have any socks left! I'm in trouble!"

Eighty-seventh floor.

"Oops. My panties and stockings vanished... This trap is so immature."

Eighty-eighth floor.

"Argh... I'm down to pants and underwear... What the heck...?!"

And then the eighty-ninth floor.

They walked a ways before discovering a trap set in front of the stairs to the floor above. Another giant panel with another armor mark.

"Argh... We have...no choice..."

Masato stepped forward onto it. The trap activated and left him standing in his underwear.

Behind him the other members followed. "Oh my!" "I knew this was coming..." They were all in the same predicament.

Then.

While Masato was refusing to turn around and busy trying to eliminate all thoughts from his mind, Shiraaase called out to him.

"Masato! Masato! A moment of your time, please."

"Wh-what is it...?"

"Next up is the ninetieth floor. The boss floor. I think a pep talk is in order. Shouldn't you turn around, face the crowd, and give us all a rousing speech?"

"Y-yeah... I would love to... Normally..."

But facing them, or even glancing backward, meant he would see things. And he would rather not see those things.

When Masato proved less than enthusiastic, Shiraaase spoke again.

"We don't mind. We need the hero's call! These things are important."

"The hero's call... That... That is my job... But... But if..."

"True. If you turn to speak to us, you will see not only we mothers but also these young girls in the altogether."

"Y-yeah... And that wouldn't be..."

"But that is a necessary evil."

"A necessary evil... Wow, that sure sounds...convincing..."

"So it should. Masato, you will be acting heroically, out of concern for your party's well-being, and whatever glimpses you catch will be necessary evil. None would blame you for it. After all, you are acting only for their benefit."

"I would be... Then... Well, if you insist..."

He wasn't doing this so he could stare at the girls. That wasn't the case at all. He was doing this for them! In which case... In which case!

"Um... S-so, everyone! There's a boss up next! Let's all focus our energies!"

Masato turned around and called out!

And when he did, he was greeted with a feast for the eyes! A young, barely clothed beauty stood before him!

"That's right. Just like Ma-kun says, there's a boss up next! Everyone, be careful!"

Young?

Well, she could certainly pass for young. She had the skin tone of a teenager, a heaping bosom snug in a lacy bra, delicate panties that left little to the imagination...

"Focus our *energies*, he said. He chose that phrasing. How infooor-mative. Heh-heh-heh."

But still, was *young* the right word? Though she was beautiful, there were certain things hinted at her age... Certainly, her propor-tions were on point, and there was no arguing that her risqué black unmentionables were a sight to behold...

But...

"We have to fight a boss now? How terrifying..."

"Yes, and in our underwear, too! ...Goodness, you certainly have kept your belly trim."

"It's all thanks to this shapewear! If I take this off, it all comes spill-ing out."

"Same here. I just can't seem to keep it tight anymore. Such a shame."

"You're so right... Look at all this extra flab around my sides!"

The rest of them were definitely not young. Probably a few decades past that.

They also seemed to be quite big on beige, and as they said, there was quite a bit of flab and overhanging bellies on display.

Whatever shame they may once have possessed had clearly long since faded away. The mob of moms weren't even trying to hide themselves behind those bags.

This was wrong, right? Yep. Super wrong.

Masato's body and soul had turned to ash. He collapsed where he stood.

"Argh... I knew better... But this is too muuuch... I stepped right in Shiraaase's traaap..."

"No, no, I intended nothing of the sort! Still... Heh-heh-heh."

While her expression was as placid as ever, that laugh proved she was thoroughly enjoying herself. Evil.

He had to recover somehow. If he could only get some sort of reward, not in a weird way, just...anything to help him get his feet back under him. But where would such a thing come—?

"You at the front! What's going on?! Get a move on!"

"What's going on...? We can't see a thing from back here!"

"Nnggg... Nnggg! I can't see anything!"

He could hear voices. The girls were somewhere in the crowd of mothers. The moms' beige lingerie barrier hid them from view.

"Argh... What are they doing...? Nobody gets it... Nobody understands... You can't be hiding back there! It isn't fair!"

"Oh my, Ma-kun, what's wrong? The stairs to the next floor are right there! You can't just stop... Oh, are you feeling sick? Should Mommy rub your belly for you?"

"Nooooo! You're the last person I needed!"

Mamako had come running over to Masato in her underwear. He was in trouble! "Ma-kun? Are you okay?" Swaying everywhere. "Don't bend overrrrrr!" He frantically scrambled away from his mother's swaying.

Masato ran like his life depended on it, right up the nearby staircase.

"I'll beat the boss and end this! If we beat it, I'm sure this hell will end!"

"Yes, let's go! Mommy is always right at your side!" *Swaaaay.*

"I'd prefer you keep your distance!!"

He was running toward the ninetieth floor—home to the stratum boss.

*   *   *

A pair of doors stood at the back of hell. Masato reached the floor with Mamako on his heels, and the count began.

Masato, Mamako, the mob of immodest moms, the girls (still out of sight).

Once everyone was accounted for, the doors opened.

"Here we go! Town mothers, step to safety! I'd appreciate it if you stay out of my sight, by which I mean nothing inappropriate! ...Ah! Shiraaase, you go wherever."

"So I shall. I can offer no assistance here. I shall watch over you from a position that offers no influence whatsoever."

"Please do! ...And our heaviest hitter is ready to go!"

"Hee-hee! Ma-kun's mommy is always ready! Also... Wise, Medhi!" she called.

In response:

"Okay! The ultimate Sage is here! My magic will save the day!"

Wise came marching forward, hand on her pink-striped panty-clad hip, a camisole enveloping her nearly flat chest.

Then...

"Leave Cura, support, and bash damage to me! I'll show you what a Melee Healer can do!"

There stood Medhi, in underwear of the purest white. She waved her staff dramatically, causing her chest to sway this way and that.

Finally, some actual girls!

"Yes! That's what I'm talking about! No more mothers! Geez! Wise, Medhi! What were you waiting for?" Masato fumed.

"Uh... I don't really get why Masato's so mad..."

"Er, um... Should we be apologizing?"

"Apologies would be acceptable!"

So ""Th-then...we're sorry?"" "Thank you!" he got apologies from both of them and deemed it settled. He'd calmed down enough to forgive.

And now that he'd calmed down...

"Huh? Like...I'm just looking right at you both and...there's no punishment or...?"

"Oh… Um… Yeah… Like, at first I was hiding and doing the whole 'look and you die' thing, but…when I saw how unconcerned all the moms were, I just kinda stopped caring."

"If nobody else cares and we're being all sensitive about it, that's just awkward. When everyone else is dancing, go dance, too, I suppose."

Human instincts were prone to matching their surroundings.

"…It's that simple?"

"Pretty much. As long as you don't think or say anything weird, we're good. So you need to start by apologizing for bringing it up at all."

"Uh, yeah, then…sorry for making it weird."

"Cool."

Apologize, be forgiven. Thank you? Was this his lucky day?

Nah, really he was more worried about their state of mind. I mean, feeling comfortable in their undies because of a bunch of moms?

"Ma-kun! The door's about to open!"

"Whoa, the boss fight! Focus! …Porta, make sure you're somewhere safe!"

"R-right! I'll be with the town moms!"

He watched—but like, not in a weird way—as Porta ran off, a giant bag on her back, the frills on her bunny panties bouncing.

This was a battle. Time to get serious.

They were on the ninetieth floor. The boss will be pretty strong…

All of them had their defense down to nothing. How could they fight like this?

Defeat it without getting hit. No other options. They had to attack first. Masato readied Firmamento, waiting for his chance to attack with everything he had.

And when the doors fully opened, what appeared…

"Heh-heh-heh. You all came as promised! That's the only praise you'll get from me!"

…was Amante.

She appeared wholly confident in her adorable floral underwear. She had a pretty great figure, after all. Wise was no competition up top, but Amante was a little smaller than Medhi. I suppose that's not really something to dwell on, though.

"Wait, you're the boss? And why are you in your underwear, too?"

"Huh? My underwear? What are you—? Aiieeeee!! Why am I in my underwear?! What the—?! ...Oh, right, I climbed up here from the eighty-first floor, so of course this happened!"

"How did you not notice?! You really are an idiot!"

"Sh-shut up! Even I'm starting to agree! Argghh!"

Whether she was easily embarrassed or just, like, having a normal reaction, Amante hastily hid herself behind the door. Only her bright red face poked out from behind.

"Um, um... I-I'm impressed you made it this far! That's the only praise you'll get from me!"

"It is an honor to receive praise from you. However, you did already say that."

"I can say it as many times as I like! Quit trying to trip me up! ...Anyway, as promised, we're gonna settle this! I'm gonna gather all my forces and totally destroy you! Come on out!"

At Amante's order, the shadows beyond the door shifted.

A number of monsters emerged. First...the body of a man, the face of a lizard—a lizardman. Next...the body of a man, the face of a wolf—a werewolf.

There followed a frog, a bird, a bear, a deer—all humanoid monsters with faces of different animals, thirty of them in total.

And all these monsters were equipped with armor like high-rank adventurers.

When he saw this, Masato swore under his breath. This was bad news.

"So they're the ninetieth-floor bosses? Definitely not your average monsters... But a mob boss? Not being able to focus on a single opponent can be rough... What now—?"

As he tried to devise a strategy, Mamako interrupted.

"Don't worry, Ma-kun. Mommy's attack can take care of any number of enemies."

"Hmm. Right... Then if we leave this to your two-hit multi-target attack—"

"Oh, you're gonna attack them? Are you? Go ahead. Attack away. Mwa-ha-ha!"

Amante seemed to be having a suspiciously good time despite still hiding behind the door.

Masato glared at her, wondering what was up, but a staring contest would get them nowhere. He figured it was best to have Mamako attack and ask questions later.

But then...

"E-excuse me! Can we have a word?"

...Pocchi's mom came scuttling over to them.

"Wh-what is it? ...This isn't about locking up or laundry, is it?"

"Of course not! Nothing of the sort. I just want a better look at those monsters' heads!"

"Those monsters'...heads?"

Pocchi's mother pointed at one of the monsters, a gorilla with a Mohawk. *What about that Mo—?*

"...Huh?"

It suddenly dawned on him. Maybe they did look familiar... *Very* familiar.

"That Mohawk...looks a lot like Pocchi's..."

"Doesn't it? That's what I thought! I've never seen anyone but my boy with such a silly hairdo!"

"Y-yeah... I've never seen one in real life on anyone else, either... It's...exactly the same. Like, that *is* Pocchi's Mohawk. But..."

But that didn't mean this gorilla with a Mohawk was Pocchi. It was just a monster. How could it be Pocchi?

Fortunately, there was an idiot happy to explain before anyone even asked the question.

"It's only natural some of you think these monsters look familiar! After all, these monsters are what became of the adventurers who placed themselves under my control!"

"Huh? ...W-wait, Amante! What did you just say?!"

"I didn't say a thing! Pocchi and them just showed up yesterday, acting like they were gonna defeat me, so I used the power of darkness to turn them and all the other adventurers into monsters! But I'd never tell you that! It'll be way more fun to have you fight in ignorance of the truth!"

"Oh, I see! You've got a lotta nerve!"

So this group of monsters were all the town's adventurers, Pocchi included.

This news came as a shock to the assembled mothers. They stared in horror, their minds refusing to accept it.

Masato gritted his teeth.

Damn! This is awful! The worst thing that could happen!

From what Amante had said at the guild, he'd been prepared for the possibility that Pocchi's goons had rejoined the enemy. But it had never occurred to him that they might have been turned into monsters.

What now?

"Um, Ma-kun! If those monsters are the village children, I can't attack them!"

"Yeah, I know! No attacking! But...what else can we do...?"

They couldn't hurt them. That much was clear. These were the town's adventurers. Was there a way to turn them back? They needed to figure that out somehow, but...

...before they could start searching for a way, Amante took action.

"What are you hesitating for? Aren't you gonna fight? How boring! Then we'll get things started! ...Come on, monsters! Get them! Tear apart Mamako, her party, and the mothers you all loathe with your bare hands!"

Amante's merciless order prompted the adventurer monsters to...

...do nothing. They all just stood right where they were.

Not only did they not fight, they all started dropping their weapons.

"Ma...maaaa... Help... Heeeellllp...meeee..." the gorilla said in a strained, almost inaudible whisper. There were tears in his eyes.

Monster Pocchi set them all off. All the adventurer monsters were soon calling for their mothers. "Moooooo...mmm..." "Maaaa... maaa..." The mothers and Masato's party could barely make out the adventurer monsters' cries, but they were repeating them, their hands reaching out for salvation.

Masato and the others just stared, stunned.

Until Amante's anger broke the silence.

"Wait! Why are you begging your mothers for help?! I thought you all hated your mothers! ...Argh... No matter! I'll just do this!"

Amante produced a palm-sized dark jewel—where had she been hiding *that*?—and threw it in the air above her.

As it spun, the jewel emanated an ominous glow bright enough to reach the ceiling high above the ninetieth floor. A huge magic circle appeared above them.

It was a sinister circle with a gloomy radiance. Bizarre symbols and pictograms lining the edges made it very clear this was nothing holy.

All concern shifted from the adventurer monsters to this magic circle. Masato took a firm grip on his sword, glaring at the ceiling.

"Hey, hey, hey! The heck is this? …Amante! Explain!"

"Why do I have to explain everything?! This is a brainwashing spell! I'll forcibly overwrite the NPC behavior and—"

But before her explanation ended, the spell activated.

A dark light shot out of the magic circle. Black liquid began falling like drops beading on the ceiling of a bathhouse.

These drops fell on the adventurer monsters and clung to their bodies as they whispered:

"Annoying… Frustrating… Infuriating… Awful. Just being around them makes you sick."

"All they ever do is scold and lecture. Do this, do that. Who cares?"

"Who is it who makes you feel like that? That's right. Them."

"They're nothing but trouble. All they do is rob their children of any peace and freedom… That's why…"

The horrible voices grew silent. The drops vanished.

Their eyes now turned unquestionably hostile, the adventurer monsters picked up their weapons and stepped forward.

"They're ready to fight! Everyone, look out!"

Masato's party prepared for battle.

But the adventurer monsters never looked at them. They scattered, racing around and past them.

"Uh… W-wait… If they're not after us, then…!"

The adventurer monsters were running directly toward the crowd of stunned mothers.

They were after their moms. Each monster targeting their own mother.

"Ah-ha-ha-ha! That's right! That's how it should be! Get them! …Meanwhile, I'm going to put some clothes on! A temporary retreat for a wardrobe change!"

Seizing her moment, Amante ran off.

Masato wanted to grab her, but this situation was far more urgent.

"Dammit! She brainwashed them into attacking their moms! This is insane!"

"We can't let them do that! Let's do something!"

"Yeah, I know! First, let's have Mom attack to slow them… No, that won't work. The stray bullets will hit the moms! Damn! What else can we do?"

Run out and help the closest ones? Starting where?

No matter which way Masato went, behind his back some other mother would be attacked by her child, screaming.

And the longer he stood still, the closer that came to reality.

He had to act swiftly. But the desire to save all of them was shackling him, leaving him unable to act at all. Then…

"…*Spara la magia per mirare… Barriera!* And! *Forte Vento!*"

"Following up! …*Spara la magia per mirare… Cieco!*"

…three spells activated in rapid succession.

First, a defensive effect. Targeting the moms, it created a magic wall in front of them.

An instant later, a powerful wind started blowing. This blew away the adventurer monsters just before they attacked the mothers.

Before they had a chance to get back up, they were hit with a status effect. All light was stolen from their eyes, leaving them totally blind. This way, they couldn't target the mothers.

This magnificent display of magic came from Wise and Medhi.

"Ha-ha! Take that! How's that for a magic girl combo?!"

"It does little but buy us time, but it's a start!"

"Well done, both of you! …Now—"

"Time to split up!"

This was no time to insist that he be the one to give directions.

"Mom, you have a plan?"

"Yes. Leave the rampaging children to their mothers… Let these moms show how amazing they can be. Hee-hee."

"That doesn't seem like a thing I need to watch, but sure, let's do that!"

"Which means we need to do something about the magic circle on the ceiling!"

"That's the cause of this calamity! If we can remove that, things might resolve themselves! …The problem is…how?"

"I've got an idea there! Leave this to me! This is my chance to shine! …Secret plan, activate! I summon Porta! Porta, over here! Hurry!"

"C-comiiiiing! I'm on my waaaay!"

Threading her way through the thrashing monsters, Porta somehow made it safely to them. Now they were all together.

They split into two groups, putting the plan into action.

Blinded, the adventurer monsters were stumbling around, bumping into one another, howling at unseen foes—their attacks hit nothing.

But the status effect limiting their actions would soon run out. Once they could see, their berserk rage would focus on their mothers, and they would once more bare their fangs.

The mothers were sitting down, trembling, waiting for that moment to arrive. For once, their ceaseless gossip had stopped. They were leaning against one another, holding hands, faces pale and downcast.

Until Mamako spoke to them.

"Everyone, I have something to say." Mamako was letting her feelings show. "I'm sure you're all frightened. I'm sure you can't believe what's happening. For your own child to be turned into a monster and attack you… Even in our worst nightmares, we've never imagined anything like this… But it is the truth. What's happening right now is very real. We must face that fact."

"…B-but this is only because that Amante girl did something to them, right?"

"Y-yes! The power of darkness! That dark jewel! That's to blame! If it weren't for that, no child would ever attack their mothers!"

Several mothers were focused on blaming the external cause.

But Mamako shook her head.

"Certainly, this strange magic had a powerful influence… But I doubt that was all. I believe these children had feelings like this to begin with. They may not have hated their parents, but they were certainly harboring feelings of dissatisfaction."

No person could accept absolutely everything about another. Large or small, there was always something not to like.

Especially when it came to those closest to you, to someone you dealt with on a daily basis, like a mother.

"Of course, I'm sure we can all say the same thing ourselves. I often sense such feelings in my own son... Just as parents have feelings, children have feelings of their own. Sometimes those frustrations bellow up, turn on us, and attack like wild monsters."

"W-well... Yes... That has happened..."

"My child used to gripe about me all the time... And I argued back, we had a huge fight, and then they ran out of the house..."

"But what's happening now is nothing out of the ordinary. These dissatisfied feelings have grown more than usual and surfaced, but these are but a part of your children. That's why..."

"We must accept it."

Mamako stood firm, poised to face any threat head-on.

"When children bare their raw emotions to us, and we argue with them, the conflict makes everything erupt. That's exactly why we must first accept their emotions, draw them to us, and then talk about it, each party making their feelings clear. What better means of resolving things could there be?"

"Accept them and talk to them...?"

"Th-that is a good approach, but..."

The mothers looked nervously at their children.

These children were built like grown-ups. They towered over their mothers, and physically they were much stronger. On top of that, they'd been turned into monsters.

How could one go about accepting such children? It seemed impossible. The mothers grew downcast again, all lost in silence.

"Don't worry! You can do it! Mothers have incredible power!"

Mamako cried, clasping her hands to her chest. A ball of light appeared before them. Its bright shine pierced through the gloom, bathing all in the warmth and kindness of A Mother's Light.

She raised the ball of light above her, and it shattered, each piece flying to one of the assembled mothers.

And the moment each accepted it...

"Eek! Wh-what is this...?!"

...the balls of light stretched out like ribbons, winding themselves around the women's bodies and limbs, until they were covered in full-body armor.

Strong armor, like a Heavy Knight's.

But this wasn't full armor—it was full ar*mom*—indestructible armor able to withstand any attacks from their children.

From bright colors to animal prints, this full armom reflected the fashion sense of the wearers. The moms had been promoted from a mom mob to Moms-at-Arms.

"This is a mother's power... Our power..."

"If we have this power, then...maybe..."

Perhaps they could accept their children's rage. One by one, their faces lit up.

Their hopes were coming true. Mamako nodded, confirming as much.

"I know you can do it," she said. "After all...you're mothers!"

"That's right! We'll show our children what we can do when it really matters!"

"We will! Mothers are always there when our children need us!"

"We'll face our children! Let us show them what mothers are made of!"

The mothers roared and formed a single line, ready to accept.

The adventurer monsters began to move. Their blindness vanished, and they began searching for their targets.

"...Gori? Goraaaaaaa!"

Bellowing, the Mohawk gorilla, Pocchi, attacked. He raised his sword, charging forward.

Pocchi's mother stepped advanced to meet him, her full armom sporting a wicked leopard print.

"You're Pocchi! I'd know you anywhere! After all, I'm your mother!"

"Gorilllaaaaaaaaaaa!"

Body, heart, and language all far too gorilla-y, Pocchi's sword slashed mercilessly. It struck his mother in her shoulder…and snapped in two. Quite easily.

"Gorii?! Go-go-goriii?!"

"Your attacks can't hurt me! Now it's Mommy's turn!"

"Go?! Gorilllllllaaaaaaaaaa?!"

Pocchi's mother reached out her arms and wrapped them tightly around gorilla Pocchi. She wasn't letting go. No matter what.

And in his mother's arms, a miracle occurred.

The moment the warmth of her maternal love embraced him, his monstrous fur vanished, and he was human once more—Pocchi was back to normal.

"Wha…?! Hey! Heeyyyyyy!"

"Don't worry. Mommy understands. You were just a little upset with me, right? I know. I understand."

"Upset?! This situation is the most upsetting thing!"

"Yes, yes. Tell me everything. I'll listen properly. We'll always be together like this so I can listen."

"You aren't listening at all, though! I just want you to let go!! Arghh… Okay, okay! I'll never do it again! Just please forgive meeeeee!"

Pocchi struggled far more than he had as a monster, letting out a cry of genuine desperation… But no, no, that couldn't be. He was in his mother's arms and just embarrassed by her affection. Probably. Let's hope so.

Similar events were happening all around. Mothers were accepting their child's attacks and giving them big ol' hugs. "Hissssssss?" "Don't worry, it's okay." "Whyyyyy?!" "Relax, Mommy understands." Even when the adventurer monsters turned human again, the mothers kept their arms tight around them, rubbing heads and backs, telling them what good children they were.

Mamako watched, smiling.

"Hee-hee. All such happy families! Good!"

She adorably pumped her fist.

*   *   *

Meanwhile, the magic circle team:

"Mamako did it again, huh? Nice."

"The strength of mothers. Magnificent."

"All I saw was a ferocious hellscape, but... Whatever. It's not happening to me."

And if it wasn't his problem, it was actually pretty entertaining. He left that part unsaid, but the grin on Masato's face was unmistakable. Anyway.

"Will it be good? It'll be good! A good item...done!"

"Oh, it's ready?"

Porta was done with Item Creation.

Masato ran over and found a crystal bomb in front of her.

"Hmm... It looks exactly the same..."

"Porta, will this work for the plan?"

"Yes, it will! I made all twenty-one crystal bombs into one! It's twenty-one times as powerful!"

"Wow... Twenty-one times as powerful as a bomb that can level a castle wall..."

They'd used the crystal bomb Pocchi had left behind in his salesman guise and the ones placed around town before the afternoon attack. Every single bomb.

"Now all I have to do is take the crystal trigger for this bomb..."

Masato carefully picked up the crystal bomb, and he was ready to go.

"Then I'll start... *Spara la magia per mirare... Colpire!*" Medhi chanted.

The spell's effect dramatically increased the accuracy of Masato's attacks.

"Me next! ...*Spara la magia per mirare—*"

"W-wait! I'm not ready—!"

"There's no time for that! Flying enemies are your domain! We're trusting you here, so get it right! ...*Barriera!* And! *Forte Vento!*"

Wise's chain cast activated: first, a defensive wall at Masato's back.

An instant later, an incredible wind sprang up. It hit him right in the

back, pulling his legs off the floor and hoisting him high into the air.
I'm flyyyyying!

"Whoooooooooa!! So much wind pressure! So much feeeeeeear!!"

A reverse bungee jump (sans bungee cable) sent Masato rocketing toward the ceiling. What. Fun. Yet, the tears were streaming. The wind pressure hurt. Oh... How was the landing gonna work? He hadn't thought this through.

And he didn't have time to think about it now. The enemy was right before him: a giant enemy in the form of a large magic circle oozing black liquid.

"Right! Then here goes the heroic blow! ...Take this!"

Masato flung the crystal bomb at the center of the magic circle. With his accuracy buffed, the crystal bomb went right where he wanted it... and Masato quickly yanked the trigger out of his pocket and pressed it. The countdown started.

The crystal bomb let out an earsplitting wail, gave off a blinding light...and detonated.

A shock wave spread, violently compressing the air. This was followed by a wall of fire, burning away the sinister artifice.

"Yessss! I did it! ...W-wait... The fire's coming right at—?!"

Masato was swallowed by the explosion and instantly burned to a crisp.

Mom's Guild Daily Report

Occupation: WMC (World Ma-kun Championship) Victor

Name: Mamako Oosuki

Business Report:

I had my first face-off with Amante, the leader of the Libere Rebellion. Amante seems to be quite good at housework and did a great job with both the dishes and the laundry. I wanted to tell her how delighted I was by this, but I wasn't about to let her beat me, especially when it came to washing Ma-kun's shirts, so I came at her with everything I had!

Other Notes:

I made a list of things you must consider when washing shirts. I recommend using a laundry net when putting a shirt in a washing machine. This will minimize wrinkles and prevent buttons from coming off. It is not necessary when washing shirts with a Holy Sword. When hanging shirts out to dry, make sure to give the fabric a good tug, stretching all the wrinkles out. This will make it much easier to iron once they've dried. Give it a try!

Member Comments:

The other notes are so completely unnecessary I can't even.

Maybe I should give this a shot.
Not for Masato or anything, though. /s

I see how that works. Wise is basically a washboard, so...
H-hey, stop it! What are you—?!

Wise took Medhi outside, and they never came back!

The Cleric Medhi chanted a spell.

"...*Spara la magia per mirare... Rianimato!*"

Light poured out of the raised staff and rained down on the coffin in front of them.

The coffin opened. Masato was resurrected, and he looked nonplussed.

"Hmm... Underestimating the force of the explosion was quite the miscalculation."

"Dying from your own plan is certainly something, Sucky Calculation Hero."

She wasn't wrong, but he didn't really need Wise giving him any new names.

"Sorry! I tried too hard when I was making it!" "Oh, no, don't worry about it."

If he pressed this point, Porta was also gonna look sad, so he dropped it.

"So...did I miss anything?"

Masato looked around.

They were still in the ninetieth-floor boss room.

Blowing up the magic circle seemed to have counted as beating the boss. The doors were open... And hey, everyone had their gear back. Dang. Never mind. Anyway.

Pocchi was prostrating himself before his mother.

"I can't apologize enough!" *Bow.*

"That's right. If you do something bad, first thing to do is say you're sorry. Apology accepted."

Pocchi's mother wasn't about to give him a hard time. She gave his

Mohawk a ruffle. It reminded Masato of himself and Mamako and was definitely making old wounds ache.

Similar interactions were happening all around them. "Sorry, Mama!" "No, it was my fault, too!" "Mom! Mercy!" "Geez, are you seriously my kid?" Different ways of apologizing and different ways of accepting it, but all of them were ending in smiles.

Looks like the monsterization of the town adventurers had ended well.

"Oh, Ma-kun! You're alive again! I'm so glad!"

"Augh! Why are you here?! I liked it better when you weren't!"

Mamako had come racing over and given him a huge hug, squeezing his face relentlessly against her. "Mmff?!" Soft. Warm. Smells nice. Can't breathe. The definition of a mom hug.

"Gaaaah! Mom! How many times have I asked you not to do that?!"

"Oh, Ma-kun, you don't need to be embarrassed! You did very well, and you've earned yourself a nice relaxing cuddle. Go right ahead and indulge!" She started rubbing his head.

"It's not an indulgence! And you know I've been trying not to indulge! I've even been skipping dessert! ...Argghh, what am I even talking about?!"

Masato pried himself from Mamako's grasp.

Time to gather intel. Masato's party gathered around the Pocchi family.

"Pardon me, Pocchi. Can we talk?"

"Uh, sure... I s'pose I owe you an explanation."

Pocchi turned from his mother toward them, straightening himself.

"Mom probably explained everything, but basically, I gathered up everyone who'd got away and came back here to take Amante down."

"Why did you—?"

"Simple. I thought we had to do something about that idiot... Y'know what wish Amante's tryin' to have granted up there?"

"Uh, no..."

"Then I'll tell ya. That idiot's gonna ask for one thing: 'I wish there were no mothers in this world.'"

"Huh...?"

Amante wanted to make it so there were no mothers?

Masato was at a loss for words. He just stared at Pocchi in disbelief.

"Stupid, right? But she's dead serious... And so were we. We had this big fight and ran away, and then we bumped into her and she started tellin' us about it. She was so excited, and it seemed kinda fun, so we got on board."

"B-but...you changed your minds, right? You went home and made up with your mothers?"

"Yeah, basically. Thanks to Mamako, we woke up, I guess, and... really missed being home. So we went back, got a looooong lecture, and then Mom started making dinner. Just a simple veggie stir-fry, only soy sauce for seasoning."

"P-Pocchi! You don't need to describe it like that! It makes it sound like I'm a lousy cook!"

"What? I didn't say it was bad. I'm just saying that was my mom's cookin'," he said, his smiling face settling his mother down. "That's right! That's our cooking. No good or bad about it. It's what hits home."

Everyone had a flavor like that in mind.

"And the bath was the same. Not some fancy hot spring. Always way too hot so it'll still be warm for the next person. But that's how it always was, how I grew up... Same with the bed. It wasn't nothin' fancy, but it was just right. And I was asleep before I knew it."

The home you grew up in had so many things like that.

You didn't even have to look. They were just everywhere.

"And I just got to thinking... I dunno how to say this...but...it's all 'cause of Mom, y'know? Only my mom can do that."

The food his mom made. The way his mom did things. That's why it felt so right.

An essence only Mom could provide.

"So if all moms vanished from the world, I couldn't have that. And I couldn't let that happen. So..."

"So you came back here to stop Amante from making her wish?"

"I did... We totally messed that up, though."

They'd ended up turned into monsters and attacking their moms. Pocchi scratched his head, ashamed of himself.

"I never thought it'd get that bad... When we reached the tower, we talked everyone else here into joining us. Ended up with thirty front-line adventurers fighting Amante together. And she turned the tables on us..."

"Huh? ...W-wait, you had thirty against one, but you still couldn't beat Amante?"

"Yeah, exactly... There's somethin' weird about her strength... I ain't talking better stats or nothin' like that... I think if she wanted to she could totally clear this tower all on her own..."

"Wow, really?"

This last line wasn't from any of them.

They turned toward the voice...and saw Amante standing in the open doorway. She'd retreated to change clothes and had only just returned.

"I could totally clear this tower all on my own... I could! I'm strong! The hundredth-floor boss can't do squat to me...in which case...!"

Even though she'd just got here, Amante turned around and ran off up the stairs beyond the door. Was she seriously going for the solo clear?

Then she'd make her wish at the top of the tower...and all mothers in the world would vanish.

They couldn't let that happen.

"Yo! Wait, Amante! Dammit! We've gotta hurry!"

Masato checked on the guild members.

Mamako, Wise, Medhi, Porta, and himself were all ready to go.

But the mothers weren't looking so hot. They were new to dungeon exploring in the first place, and with the shock of their children's transformation and attacks, they all seemed exhausted. None of them looked like they were getting up anytime soon. Some were upright only because their kids were supporting them. These moms could never leave like this...

Then Shiraaase, who was looking after them, called out.

"I'll take care of them. Masato, you and your party go on ahead!"

"Thanks! ...But wow, you're actually cooperating voluntarily?"

"If I do nothing here, then it will be like I only came here to do a striptease on the tower traps. I'll take advantage of the admin system rights to send everyone else back out of the tower."

"Glad you weren't into that sort of thing! ...All right, everyone!"

"Okay! Let's go!"

"We're totally set! Let's hurry!"

"I have the perfect item ready! This will let us move faster!"

"Thank you, Porta! That's so helpful!"

"Great! Come on!"

They ran off through the doors.

"I'm countin' on you guys!" Pocchi yelled after them, fist raised. "You're the only ones who can save our moms!"

They ran up the stairs after Amante.

Once the hero's party was out of sight...

"Now then, one job to do before we move everyone," Shiraaase muttered. She scanned the floor around her, searching for something nearby...

There—the dark jewel.

"Our first time securing one of these undamaged. And we've positively identified the user... As soon as we have her in custody, we'll conduct a thorough investigation into the dark item, changing NPCs into monsters and altering the ninetieth-floor boss."

Shiraaase scooped up the dark jewel, wrapped it in cloth, and slipped it into her pocket. Evidence secured.

But just then...

"*Haahh, haahh*... I—I forgot to mention! You may have turned those monsters back into adventurers, but that doesn't mean Mamako Oosuki won! The winner of this contest will be whoever reaches the top first... Huh?"

Amante was standing at the base of the stairs, panting.

She looked around, confused.

"W-wait... Um... If Mamako Oosuki and her party aren't here, then..."

"I believe the ones you're looking for just went up the stairs you're standing on... Did you not run into them?"

"Huh? No, didn't see any sign of... C-crap! I'd better go after them!"

Amante turned and raced back up the stairs.

Shiraaase watched her leave impassively.

"With Mamako not here, she certainly could have brainwashed all the adventurers here again...but if even that doesn't occur to her...I'm not sure we'll really learn anything of value interrogating someone so stupid."

Shiraaase could be quite mean sometimes.

The stratum starting from the ninety-first floor could not be more different from the hellscape below.

Simply put, this was a heavenly palace: vast spaces built out of beautiful porcelain-white material, flowers blooming all around, detailed carvings covering the pillars and walls, murals praising the gods on the ceilings above. A carpet laid out on the polished floors.

This place had a divine aura quite unlike the more dungeon-y sections below. The sort of place where you wanted to stand still and let soak in... Unfortunately, time was of the essence.

"Hurry! Everyone, keep running!"

Masato's party sped across the floors of heaven.

It might look like heaven, but this was still a dungeon. There were still monsters.

But they didn't care. And this time, it wasn't because Mamako was with them.

"Your item's amazing, Porta! We're not running into any monsters! That effect is crazy strong!"

"For real! ...Um, what was it called again...?"

"It's Thou Dost Not Wish to Fight water!"

"Normally, it just lowers the encounter rate a little, but with Porta's Item Creation, the effect is so strong we aren't seeing any enemies at all!"

"Um, there are enemies, but they don't notice us, and we can't see them! So it's safe for us to just keep going!"

"You're amazing, Porta! So clever!"

"Th-thank you!"

So.

"Then let's get a move on! ...Y'know, I felt like something whizzed past us earlier... I guess it was a monster... Or maybe Amante...?"

"No way. I mean, she said she was one of the Four Heavenly Kings, right? She's, like, a boss or something. Don't see why an item designed to let us avoid normal fights would work on her."

"Good point... Unless the settings accidentally had her designated as a trash mob or something. Which would just be sad. So we're bound to bump into her!" replied Medhi.

"Yeah! We gotta be ready for a fight whenever, Porta!" said Masato.

"Yes! I'll do everything I can! Everyone else, conserve your strength!"

Poor Amante.

Porta was in the lead, scattering the contents of a vial dramatically labeled THOU DOST NOT WISH TO FIGHT! Their safe passage was assured. The party progressed without interruption. "...Oh, a jump tile!" They bounded upward, surging ahead.

The group reached the ninety-seventh floor.

"Still no sign of Amante... Is she farther ahead or wandering around nearby? ...Oh, found the stairs! Sweet!"

They spied the stairs to the ninety-eighth floor. There were a hundred floors in all, so only three left.

If they couldn't find Amante, then they could just reach the top first and take her down when she caught up. Not slowing down for a second, they went up the stairs, pressing onward.

"Whoa, what the...?"

The ninety-eighth floor: a very simple layout with just a single long corridor.

But there was a magic circle drawn in the middle of it, so large they couldn't get past without stepping on it.

"That's clearly bad news... A final difficulty spike before the last boss... But no point in hesitating... Let's just charge on through!"

Letting momentum take them, they tried to run straight across the magic circle.

A moment later, they all vanished.

Masato found himself standing at the end of a corridor.

"...Uh... Huh?"

It was made of stone, just like the lower floors. But this was much smaller. Only two or three people could walk through side by side.

And Masato was the only one here. There were no signs of his party. Was this...?

"Ohhh... Oh, yeah, yeah. I get it. One of these."

Masato knew what was going on.

"Classic dungeon design. RPGs do this all the time. You start clearing a dungeon together, step on a trap, and all get thrown to separate areas!"

Yep. Clearly that. No proof, but what else could it be?

"But annoying as it is, we just each have to clear our bit of dungeon and we'll be together again. We'll all make it just fine! Obviously. That's how these things work! That's the point!"

His voice was a little tense and maybe a bit too loud considering he was talking to himself. He was mostly trying to keep the fear at bay. To push back a wave of anxiety.

He couldn't let it get to him.

"...Right! Let's move!"

Masato slapped himself across his cheeks, trying to fire himself up, and began walking forward. He'd better draw his sword and be ready for a fight... Nah, it'd be no good to be all cowardly. "Okay! Let's move!" he shouted again.

It was a very simple layout. Just a single path leading straight ahead. Humming loudly like he normally never would, desperately trying to cheer himself up, he walked along it.

After a while, he found a side passage.

"Oh, come on! You can't give me branches now! ...Wait... Is someone there?"

They were hidden behind the corner, but he could see a shadow on the floor. He wasn't scared. Definitely not. But his knees were shaking a bit. And when he called out...

The person stepped out of hiding, a huge smile on her face.

"Hee-hee! Ma-kun, I found yooou!"

It was Mamako—her face, her voice, definitely her. **Mommy appeared!**

Masato let out a sigh so dramatic his insides nearly came out with it.

"Geez... Moooooooom... Don't scare me like thaaat..."

"Sorry! I didn't mean to! Hee-hee."

"Don't 'hee-hee' me! Gawd, so annoying! ...Anyway, looks like you're safe and everything, so that's good... Let's keep moving!"

Masato complained quite loudly but said how he really felt quite softly—keeping his relief a secret.

His posture remarkably improved. He started walking again with nothing to fear. Not that he was scared to begin with, obviously.

He stepped forward, passing the side passage.

"So if you're here, Mom, then the other three... Huh?"

He turned to address her, assuming she'd joined him, but she clearly hadn't.

She was staring at him from around the corner of the side passage. Still with that broad smile.

"Hee-hee. Ma-kun, not that way. This way. Come over here."

"Huh? Oh, that's the way to go? You could've said something first, for cryin' out loud."

Masato turned back and was about to start down the side passage...

But it was a dead end.

"...So not this way, then."

"No, you're right where I want you. Come, Ma-kun. This way."

Mamako was beckoning to him.

But that was clearly the wrong way. Something was off here.

"...Hmm."

An idea was forming in his mind. Masato picked up a pebble off the ground and tossed it down the passage behind Mamako.

It bounced a couple of times and then SCHUNK! "Whoa!" Iron bars slammed down from above, turning the side passage into a prison cell.

"Y-yo, what the—?! ...Oh, never mind. I get it."

"My, my! I was so close to catching you, Ma-kun. Too bad!"

Behind the bars, Mamako kept on smiling like Mamako. The one saving grace was that she hadn't suddenly transformed into a monster or anything.

And yet, she was one.

"A trap, huh?"

If he'd listened to his fake mother and stepped into that passage, the doors would have come slamming shut and he'd be at Game Over.

Right.

"Oh, Ma-kun! Mommy's right here! This way! Hee-hee."

There was another side passage ahead of Masato and another Mamako in it. Masato's mother was not the sort of mother who could make doppelgangers of herself... No, he could totally see her doing that somehow if the situation called for it. Point was, this Mamako was a fake. Masato did not have two moms.

"Ma-kun, you must be tired. Come rest here. Look, there's a futon and everything! Mommy will pat the futon down for you..."

"I hear you shouldn't do that," he said, walking right past her. "Bad for the cotton inside."

Not even worth a sideways glance.

Yep, a trap. See?

"Ma-kun!" "Hey, Ma-kun! It's Mommy!" "Maaa-kuuuun!" "Over here!"

As Masato moved forward, he passed one side passage after another, each one with a different Mamako cooing for his attention. He ignored them all.

"Geez, who has time for this? Gimme a break."

The fake Mamakos never came out of the side passages. It seemed like their movements were limited to those cells. As long as he didn't step inside and just walked right past them, he'd be fine.

So he did.

"...Oh, is that the exit?"

He saw a staircase up ahead of him. An end at last! No more of this aggravating corridor.

He'd been unsure how he'd fare on his own, but it looked like he'd made it through unscathed. Relieved to have passed this trial, Masato glanced over his shoulder.

""""""Hee-hee. Ma-kun. You can't just leave Mommy behind.""""""

See? Nothing but Mamakos behind him.

"The horror... The unspeakable horrorrrrrrrrrrrrr!!"

The corridor behind Masato was completely filled with Mamakos.

And not just ordinary Mamakos—dark Mamakos, all with a sinister aura like Medhi during her episodes. Seriously terrifying.

The pack of dark Mamakos was hot on his heels.

"Hee-hee-hee. Say, Ma-kun, why don't you listen to Mommy? You baaad boy."

"If you don't do what Mommy says, I'll have to punish you!"

"But how, I wonder? …What about a nice hug, then some cuddling, then…"

"Bite off his head! I wonder what Ma-kun tastes like. Hee-hee."

"N-no… No… NOOOOOOOOOOOOOOOOOOOOOOOO!!"

Masato went full Munch's *The Scream*, frozen on the spot. The fear rising up from deep within left him completely paralyzed. What was so frightening? Having this many of his own mom!

And thus, Masato was gobbled up, unable to resist at all…

However.

"Ma-kun! There you are! I'm coming!"

Yet another Mamako. Here comes Mamako. This Mamako came down the stairs behind him. "Not another oooooone!" Masato screamed, snot flying everywhere.

But the moment his eyes hit her, he knew.

Oh… She's my mom… My real mom.

She looked exactly like all the other Mamakos. The expression was the only difference.

But there was something he sensed from only her. Masato had the power to sense that thing:

A Child's Sense.

Masato obtained that skill in this moment.

But sadly, Masato was not capable of noticing this skill. The situation was too dire.

All that mattered now was whether the Mamako coming down the stairs was real or not.

"Y-you're my mom, right? You're absolutely the real one?!"

"Yes, I am! I see there are lots of mommies here, but…you know which is me, don't you?"

"Yeah! I can tell! I'd know you anywhere! You're my mom!"

"That's right! So leave this to Mommy!"

"No one else pushes me aside and takes over like Mom!"

Mamako ran down the stairs, facing the mass of dark Mamakos.

She looked very grim indeed. He'd never seen her look this angry.

"How dare you… How dare you scare Ma-kun like that…! And with my face and voice…? What if you made Ma-kun afraid of me…? What if Ma-kun stopped liking me because of you…? …This is just… This is just unforgivable! I'm going to do everything I can to see that you are thoroughly scolded!"

Mamako's full-power scolding!

One hand on her hip, one finger raised in front of her!

"Tut, tut!"

Such scoldings! Mamako's most powerful mark of scorn! A genuine "Tut, tut!"

No, wait, what the heck?! Just as Masato was about to say something …

The light of anger collected in front of Mamako, compressing into a beam of light! Like a laser cannon on a spaceship, it fired!

"Aughhhhhhhhhhhhhhhhhhh!! Something crazy just came out of herrrrrr!!"

Masato could only scream, his eyes rolling up in his head.

The insane thing that shot out of Mamako swallowed up all the dark Mamakos in the corridor, filling the entire passage with a light so bright Masato didn't dare open his eyes.

When the brightness faded, nothing remained. Maybe those *tuts* were actually short for *destruction*?

"Whew, that settles that… Ma-kun, Mommy did it! Hee-hee."

Mamako's smile after firing a laser cannon was so normal it was actually pretty scary.

But then… "Hey, what happened? "There was a loud noise and a bright light!" "Mama, are you okay? …Oh, Masato!" Wise, Medhi, and Porta came running down the stairs.

"Oh! You guys are all okay! So you made it past the traps, huh?"

"Yeah. Like, tons of my mom showed up and were all like, 'Rest here!' and honestly, how obvious can you be? I just chain cast and blew 'em all to hell."

"I, too, had a large number of fake mothers, so I just used my staff to thwack them into silence. It was delightful. Heh-heh-heh."

"Um... I—I was totally fine! Nothing weird happened at all!"

"Cool, cool, glad we made it! ...But, uh, listen to this, just now..."

Masato, tears in his eyes, was about to tell them all about the laser cannon.

But just then, the corridor was suddenly rocked by a massive explosion.

"That came from above... That must be the ninety-ninth floor, so up there... *Gasp!* Oh no!"

Everyone looked at one another, already all too sure of the situation, before breaking into a run.

They raced through the dust-covered ninety-ninth floor and up the stairs at the end.

This was floor one hundred—surrounded by beautiful white walls, the floor containing the final boss.

Or at least, it should have been.

"Um... Uh-oh."

The boss was gone. Only the remains of it lingered, moments from fading away.

It had most likely been some sort of giant angelic warrior. Glowing light armor, wings, a halo over its head...all filled with holes like someone had unloaded a shotgun at it.

And the one picking it up and flinging it at the closed doors...was Amante.

"Hey! Why are they still closed?! Open at once! I said open!"

No matter how many times she slammed the corpse against the doors, no matter how many times she yelled, they would not open.

This tower was a solo killer—a tower impossible to clear on your own. Its design was absolute. There was no way she could leave by herself.

Amante had not yet reached the top. That was a relief.

But no one felt relieved. They were clearly staring at a monster.

"...She really did solo the boss."

"Yeah, I did! I kicked its ass! But the door closed while we were fighting! This door is stupid strong, and I used all the crystal bombs I had, but it didn't budge! ...Wait... Huh?"

Amante heard Masato whisper and turned toward the party.

"When did you get here?! ...F-fine, whatever! If we can't reach the top, we'll just have to finish this here! Let's do this!"

Amante pulled her sword out of the angel's neck and pointed it at them.

"We've gotta fight her? ...Honestly, this could be real rough."

"Seriously... This is a guild-focused dungeon and that was clearly the last boss... It's supposed to be impossible to solo."

"Which means she's impossibly powerful..."

"Eep... M-Mama! Amante seems really strong!"

"She does. This could be tricky... Porta, you go hide somewhere safe. If you can support us from back there, that would be lovely, but don't push yourself."

"R-right! Got it!"

Porta ran back to the stairs and hid.

The challengers forced back their trepidation and made ready. The fight could no longer be avoided.

Mamako held a Holy Sword in each hand, ready to start the fight by swinging both of them. Wise pulled out her tome, focusing her mind. Medhi had already started a chant.

At the front of the party, Masato tightened his grip on Firmamento.

"...Hey, Amante. You might be after a one-on-one fight with Mom, but if we say the third battle is worth a thousand times the points, is it cool if we join in?"

"Sure, whatever. Mamako Oosuki, of course...and Wise the Sage and Medhi the Cleric, was it? They've said a lotta crap I wanna pay them back for."

"I don't remember saying a single thing that wasn't true," remarked Wise.

"We simply stated the facts, as honest people do. This is so petty and unfair."

"Nah, you guys were pretty mean a few times...but, uh, what about me? I'm the hero, the leader, possibly your greatest threat."

"Masato Oosuki... Well... I don't feel very strongly about you one way or the other..."

"You don't?!"

"Yeah, you're just Mamako Oosuki's kid, so that sorta puts you on the list, I guess."

"I'm only your enemy because of my mom?! ...Why am I even heeeeere?!"

What was the point of his existence? He had some introspection coming.

But first, they had to fight.

"There's no way I'd just up and vanish without settling things with Mamako Oosuki. I need to crush her here and give her party a pounding while I'm at it! Get ready to lose, suckers!" Amante yelled.

And with that, she threw her thin sword high overhead. "Huh?" It spun through the air, flying toward them.

And while they were distracted by that—

"Now!"

—Amante kicked the ground and flung herself toward them, catching the group completely off guard.

"Whoa! She's fast...!!"

"Masato Oosuki! You don't matter, so you go down first!"

It was a pretty mean thing of her to say, but before Masato could complain, Amante landed her attack. The full force of her charge was concentrated in a kick aimed right at his gut.

In that instant:

"Barriera!"

Medhi had already finished her chant, and she activated her spell. A defensive wall appeared in front of Masato. "Like I'd just let you hit me!" Masato yelled, thrusting his left arm forward and deploying his own shield wall.

Now Masato had two walls protecting him.

"Those are pointless! Useless!"

But as thin as Amante's leg looked, her kick easily shattered both walls and dug deep in Masato's gut. "Guh?!" The blow threatened to obliterate both body and consciousness. Masato fell to his knees.

"Good position! I can work with that!"

Amante used Masato as a springboard to launch herself high in the air. She reached one hand out and caught her sword as it fell past her...

...aiming it right at Mamako.

"Mamako Oosuki! I'll finish you with one blow!"

"Oh... Ah...?!"

While Mamako was distracted by her son's injuries, Amante attacked from above.

But Wise was here.

"I won't let you! ...*Spara la magia per mirare... Vento Tagliare!* And! *Vento Tagliare!*"

Her chain cast spells activated. Double gale-force winds slammed against Amante. Unable to dodge in midair, the full impact hit her, pushing her far away.

"Drat! You've got a lotta nerve!"

"Ha-hah! Serves you... Wait, huh?"

The attack was successfully blocked, but a moment later, the wind suddenly reversed itself, blowing back at them. "Wah!!" "Eeek!!" Mamako and Wise were flung away. "Unh!" "Aiieeee!" Masato and Medhi were flung away with them. The wind had a hit box, and they all took damage.

Covered in cuts, Medhi yelled, "Are you insane, Wise? You just attacked your own side! Who does that?!"

"I—I didn't mean to! Seriously, I aimed that properly! Something's not right here—"

"Medhi! Wise! This is no time for arguing!"

"Yeah, save the argument for later and focus on the battle at hand! ...She's seriously tough!"

Masato glared at Amante—who appeared to be totally fine.

She'd soaked a powerful attack spell head-on without sustaining any visible injuries.

But we're covered in cuts... What's going on here?

They'd experienced her toughness firsthand after watching her survive the jump off of the Mom's Guild Hotel roof. But even so, she should have taken *some* damage. Either her magic resist was incredibly high or she had some equipment on that nulled magic... Or...

"Right, then," Medhi said. "Leave the magic attacks to me! You there, Sage who sucks at magic, watch how I fight! You just might learn a thing or two!"

"Wha...?! I do not suck! Ugh, you piss me off! ...Wait, you're a Healer! Do you even have any attack magic? You can't do it! Don't make things up!"

"Oh, I can! And I will now demonstrate! Zip it, watch, and weep!"

"Uh, hey, Medhi! Don't—"

Masato tried to stop her but was too late.

Fueled by her squabble with Wise, Medhi unleashed the dark power within her and chanted, "...*Spara la magia per mirare... Morte!*"

A specter of death appeared above Medhi's raised staff and flew directly toward Amante. "Whoa, instant death spell!" Did that count as attack magic or support magic? Could be either, but clearly, Medhi could use it. Except...

"Mwa-ha-ha, useless."

Where this reaper should have passed through its target, snatching her soul...

...it instead stopped right in front of Amante—"...Uh?"—turned around—"Huh?"—wafted back—"Wait..."—split in four—"Crap!"—and shot through the entire party.

The instant death spell activated. But Masato was unaffected. Mamako was unaffected, too. They were both wearing armor that resisted status effects and therefore managed to withstand it.

Medhi died. Wise died, too. Both went straight into their coffins.

"The heck are you guys even dooooinnggggg?!"

"Oh my goodness! How awful!"

Besties in death, it seemed like there were sobs coming from the pair of coffins lying side by side—but really, it was Masato who wanted to cry. "Uggghhh!" "Porta, sweetie, can you take care of them?" "Yes, coming!" Neither wanted to bring Porta into harm's way, but only she could Rianimato the party mages.

Masato and Mamako drew their swords, watching Amante as she walked slowly toward them.

Medhi's action had taken Wise out with her, the worst kind of self-destruct, but it had made one thing very clear.

"…So, Amante, you seem to have some nasty little powers there."

"Heh-heh-heh. Whatever do you mean? …I am one who stands against all mothers, the embodiment of rebellion! My body harbors the power to send anything you throw at me flying right back at you! In other words, I have a passive skill that reflects attacks! But you think I'm just going to tell you that?"

"You don't say? Well, thanks for explaining all that."

A passive skill that reflected damage. That was ridiculous.

"Ma-kun! Mommy's gonna attack now! Here goes—"

"No, wait, stop! Let me make sure of something first!"

He hastily restrained his mother.

Masato first tried going for some light damage as a test. Amante approached him, grinning confidently, and he stepped forward and tapped her on the shoulder.

Amante didn't even try to block it. Instead, a cut opened up on Masato's body. The damage was reflected back at Masato.

Which meant… Yep, this was beyond ridiculous and went straight into cheat territory.

"Hey… Whoa, whoa, whoa, whoa! If you reflect both magic and physical attacks, that's not even fair! We can't attack you at all!"

"Don't worry, Ma-kun! Mommy's attacking next! Here goes—!"

"Stop!! For the love of God, please, quit trying to attack!! Did you not listen to the words I just said?! If your attack gets reflected, you'll wipe us all out!!"

And they wouldn't just wipe once. They might seriously die, like, five times. Masato threw his entire weight on Mamako's arm, forcibly stopping her. "Goodness… How embarrassing! Hee-hee!" "Now's not the time for that, Mom!!" She was just happy for her son's touch, but somehow he managed to get her to back down.

Then Amante laughed. A malicious, sneering laugh.

"Seriously, moms are the worst… You agree with me, don't you, Masato Oosuki?"

"W-well, she does make life hard for me sometimes."

"That's right! That's what moms do… You'd be better off if I kill her for you. Wouldn't you?"

"Huh?! That's not true! I didn't say—"

"Once your mother's gone, you'll be free—free of all the torments she brings you, free to adventure to your heart's desire. No one getting in your way, no one making you suffer. Every day will be so great. You'll truly enjoy living inside this game for once. Right?"

"Th-that's…"

Not true, he started to say, but suddenly he couldn't quite get the words out.

Adventuring with his mother had definitely taken its toll on Masato. He had a laundry list of complaints. And it was absolutely clear that most of those were Mamako's fault.

Part of him wanted to admit Amante had a point…

"Masato! You can't let her get to you! Keep it together!" Wise yelled.

Alive again, she came running over, tome in her hand. Was she seriously going to attack again?

"Ah! No, wait, Amante is—"

"She can reflect attacks, right? I heard! But even if that's true, we can still do something! …An eye for an eye, a reflection for a reflection!"

If the enemy reflected magic, then you could attack them by reflecting spells off your allies. There were any number of games where this was a viable technique.

Wise started to chant a spell, but before she could…

"…*Spara la magia per mirare… Tacere!*"

…Amante got her spell off first. Wise was wrapped in a mist that sealed magic.

Wise's magic was sealed!

"Whaaa…?! Y-you're a Fencer! How can you use magic?!"

"I may be a Fencer, but I'm a Magic Fencer! Of course I can use magic. Not that I need to tell you what my job is! …No matter. Sage Wise! Tell me one thing."

"What?"

"I thought you despised your own selfish mother. You had a huge fight, parted ways…and if it weren't for Mamako Oosuki's meddling, you would never have even tried to patch things up with her. You could have lived a life of freedom on your own! Well?"

"W-well… I mean, how do you know about—? …Ah!"

Wise's gaze shifted to behind Amante.

Where Medhi was. Dark power fully unleashed, her expression one of total fury, her staff raised high...and swinging toward Amante's head.

But Amante didn't even turn around. She just raised her sword and easily blocked the blow.

"Wha...?! One-handed? With that flimsy blade?!"

"If I hadn't blocked it, the attack damage would have been reflected onto you. Be grateful I showed you that mercy... And, Cleric Medhi. I should ask you as well."

"Wh-what? Make it snappy!"

"Then I'll get right to the point. You resented your mother. Why wouldn't you? No mother should be as domineering as yours. You even wanted her dead! You actually tried to kill her!"

"W-well... B-but that's not true now! She changed her mind! Now she's actually putting me first—!"

"Sure, sure. That's how they pull one over on you... *Pfft*."

"Eep!!"

Amante brushed Medhi's staff away like she was swatting a fly.

She then turned her gaze on Porta, who stood a safe distance back.

"I've got nothing to say to you, Porta. You're already on my side."

"Huh...?"

Neither Porta nor the others seemed to know what she meant by that.

But Amante went on without waiting for them to figure it out.

"Adventuring with your mothers makes no sense at all. All of you agree with that much. Of course you do. It's downright insane! ...And being trapped in this insane situation had been driving you all mad."

"Hold on! We're not crazy—!"

"It's only common sense that boys and girls your age don't take baths together."

Point taken. That hit way too close to home.

"Right, Sage Wise?"

"W-well... That might be the case, but..."

"Wait! Certainly, the bath thing is a tad unusual, but that doesn't make us crazy! When we're in the bath with Masato, Mamako is always with us, which is why we can relax and—"

"Come on, Cleric Medhi. 'Mom's with us, so it's okay'? That logic doesn't even make sense! …You're with a mother, so you can take a bath with a boy or parade around in your underwear like earlier? And that doesn't seem weird to you?"

"Um… Well… It's certainly…"

"You sure had a lot to say about me, but it's like you've forgotten what being a girl is all about. And you know why? Because Mamako Oosuki is here, you're not even allowed to be a girl… Right, Masato Oosuki?"

Amante turned on him, her gaze piercing right through him.

"Masato Oosuki, you've been traveling with them. Haven't you noticed?"

"Noticed what?"

"You're adventuring with girls your own age. Normally, wouldn't you start harboring feelings for one another? Have moments that make your heart skip a beat? …Perhaps catch the scent of romance in the air? That's how these things work, no? But is that happening?"

"Well…"

Masato and Wise. Masato and Medhi. There'd been moments with each where they'd bonded. They'd met, gotten to know each other, and he'd helped them resolve their predicaments. They had their share of contacts, necessary evils or otherwise.

But had that led to any budding romance? Not really, no.

"Masato Oosuki… These girls don't even see you as a male anymore. You've sensed that before, haven't you?"

"Erk…"

He'd thought as much. When bellies were exposed, when piggyback rides were given without comment, and especially during the whole underwear parade incident.

He'd been worried about exactly that.

When she saw him at a loss for words, Amante nodded, satisfied.

"I knew it! I was right… If they saw you as a male, you'd be a potential romantic partner. But nothing like that has happened…and the reason why is clear."

"…And what reason is that?"

"Your mom's here with you. With her in tow and at your group's center, you all become a family. You stop seeing one another as members of the opposite sex."

"Family...?"

"Yes, Masato Oosuki. You get it now? ...Days spent adventuring in pursuit of love... Your mother has robbed you of that possibility. Mamako Oosuki stole that from you!"

Amante pointed her sword at Mamako, who seemed caught off guard by all this. Amante seemed sure no one would stop her attack this time...

...but Masato stepped between them.

"Stop it."

"Why would you stop me? Didn't you understand a word I said? Your destiny is all twisted out of shape, and it's your mother's fault! Because of Mamako Oosuki, nothing makes sense—!"

"So what if it doesn't?"

This wasn't apathy talking. He had clear, strong emotions backing his words.

Masato looked Amante right in the eye, no hesitation in his voice.

"We're on an adventure with my mother. An adventure nobody else has had, with so many things we haven't even begun to understand. Of course, lots of those things rattle us...and from an outsider's perspective might seem pretty weird."

He'd been brought inside a video game with his mother—and she was much, much stronger than her son, the ostensible hero.

She'd even come with him to school, something mothers should never do. And not just that—she'd put on a sailor uniform and a school swimsuit. That sort of thing happened all the time to him.

It was weird.

How many times had Masato said that same thing?

"It is weird. I totally agree! Every part of this has been weird. My mom's just insane... Even this tower quest is nuts. Forming a guild out of nothing but moms, trying to clear a dungeon with them at our heels... My mother's gotten me into all kinds of crap. It's pretty exhausting."

"So—!"

"But, you know...that's what the adventure is, I think."

A real adventure, by its very nature, did not mean following the roads everyone had already traveled.

"Even right this instant, we're in a situation nobody else has ever experienced. We don't know the right way out of it, but we're trying to get through it anyway... This right here? This is a real adventure."

Reeling with surprise in the face of unbelievable events, tormented by events his mind couldn't quite accept—

—that was an adventure. All of this was. Everything Masato had gone through.

Even as he explained this to Amante, the truth of it began to permeate his very being.

"An adventure with your mother... It's an adventure that's ours alone, one only we can have."

One of a kind. Unique. Without compare.

If he'd gotten what he thought he wanted, he couldn't have had this. This adventure could only happen here.

"So I'm gonna keep being myself and continue adventuring with my mom. Even if it's weird. We'll trust that it'll take us forward... We've got everything we need to make that happen."

He didn't need to say what that was.

Wise, Medhi, and Porta all stood by his side.

His party was with him.

"That's our answer. But...can we get a word from someone who's been uncharacteristically quiet this whole time? Or are you too touched to speak?"

Only half teasing, he called to her.

"Yes... Mommy is just so overcome... I don't know what to say!"

Mamako took her place at Masato's side.

He glanced over at her. She was smiling just like always, but her eyes were glistening. This was nothing to cry about, but mothers were prone to this sort of thing.

"Ma-kun. Wise. Medhi. Porta. Thank you so much."

"You're welcome. Especially for staying out of it for once and letting me, your son, get a chance to take center stage. Figured we might as well have ourselves an adventure together."

"No need to thank us. We didn't do anything to warrant your thanks, Mamako."

"Yes. We're all here because we chose to be."

"I think I should be the one thanking you! So thank you!"

"There you have it... Mom, as one mother, can you give Amante a piece of your mind?"

"Yes, I think I will."

Mamako took a step forward, facing Amante.

"Amante, I have something to say."

"Grr... I don't want to talk to you...but okay. I'll give you this one shot. Let's hear it."

"Okay... Amante, dear. Why are you like this? Why do you treat mothers like they're a nuisance? Do you hate yours?"

"Hmph. This is way beyond love and hate! I refuse to accept their very existence! ...What I desire is a world with no mothers... That's what I'm gonna wish for once I get to the top of the tower! 'I wish there were no mothers in the world.' Not that I have to explain that to you!"

"So you really are going to wish for something that awful... I see." Mamako sighed, frowning slightly. "...Amante, I am quite upset... Maybe you have good reasons for being like this... I'm sure you do. But even so, I can't help being angry. I can't help scolding you."

Mamako's scoldings.

That didn't sound good. "Uh, Mom?!" Masato had a bad feeling about this and tried to stop her, but... "Masato! Stay out of it!" "I'm sure Mamako knows what she's doing!" ...Wise and Medhi grabbed him, preventing him from interfering.

As he struggled, Mamako put a hand on her hip and raised an index finger.

"Gathering those runaway children, making so many mothers worry, and then making them attack their own mothers...and to top it all off, wishing to have all mothers eliminated from the world... I cannot forgive that! So I'm going to scold you, Amante! Are you ready for it?!"

"Huh? Scold me? You think I'm just gonna stand here and let you? Useless, useless! This is ridiculous."

"Then here I go! ...Aaand... *Tut, tut!*"

Masato yelled for her to stop, but his cries echoed in futility.

Mamako's focused light of fury became a massive laser and surged forth. The *tut tut* cannon of scolding!

The beam was not reflected. "Buh?" Stunned, Amante was swallowed up in it. The laser went through her and the doors behind her.

Everyone gaped in amazement, blinded by the light.

"M-Mamako shoots beams now..."

"Sh-she's literally a weapon..."

"Wow! Mama Beam! So bright! Amazing!"

"I just told you to stay out of it, and here you are butting into everythiiiiing!!"

Had Amante been destroyed? Something like this would surely do the trick, leave her totally obliterated. Good-bye, world.

No, wait, there was something left.

The light of the *tut*s passed, and Amante remained.

"Huh? ...Wait, seriously?! She survived Mom's beam?! Holy crap!"

Masato couldn't believe his eyes, but it was no illusion. Half her body was charred, her aggressive ponytail frizzled end to end, and she looked ready to topple over, but she was without a doubt still standing.

"Gah... H-how is that move so strong?! ...And I couldn't reflect it... What does that even mean?! ...What *was* that attack...?!"

"That wasn't an attack at all! I merely scolded you."

"That raised scolding to another level!! I was seriously convinced you were about to wipe me from existence, y'know?! You really are insane!! ...Ugh, I was an idiot to even try to fight you... Fine!"

Amante turned on her heel and staggered away. She was headed for the doors.

The doors were still closed, but Mamako's cannon had punched a hole through them, leaving an Amante-shaped section behind. There was still enough space on either side for a person to step through, however.

This was the tower's hundredth floor; if she went up the stairs behind those doors, she'd be...

"Ah! Wait, is she—?!"

"She knows she doesn't stand a chance against Mamako, so she's gonna use her wish to eliminate her!"

"What a sore loser! We can't let that happen!"

"Yes! We have to stop her! I'm giving chase!"

"That's right! Let's hurry!"

They all broke into a run, chasing Amante up the stairs.

Soon, they arrived at the tower's roof. There was nothing up there but a single stone slab with the words MAKE THY WISH carved into it. All that surrounded them was the sky above.

Amante reached the slab first.

"All I have to do is make my wish here, right? Very well! I wish that all mothers—"

But before Amante could make her wish:

"Not happening! I'm gonna make my wish first! ...Um, uh..."

"Yes, Ma-kun! Remember what Wise said before we came to this town! About what would happen here! Go on!"

"Huh? O-oh, right! That!"

Heeding Mamako's advice, Masato hurriedly made his wish!

"I wish we each had a freshly laid egg! ...Wait, no, not that, I didn't mean—!!"

Too late.

From far above, a pack of half a dozen eggs came drifting down and landed in Mamako's hands—one each for Mamako, Masato, Medhi, Wise, Porta, and even Amante. A farm-fresh half-dozen.

Masato's wish was granted!

"Oh my! We were just out of eggs, too! How helpful. What a nice way to end things."

Mamako was extremely pleased! This was perfect for tomorrow's breakfast!

But wait a second.

"Huh? ...Y-you're kidding, right? ... Th-that's not... That's not what I...! ...I wish there were no mothers in this world! That's my wish! Grant my wish!"

Amante grabbed the stone slab, screaming, but not only was her wish not granted, the slab sank into the floor, vanishing without a trace.

"N-no... My wish... I finally had my chance... Six fresh eggs? What even—?! ...Argghh! This is why I haaaaate mothers!!"

Amante fled down the stairs, sobbing.

Meanwhile...

"I've gotta learn to think before I speak... Please, fix that for me... Fix it..."

...tears flowing down his cheeks, Masato made a new wish of his own—but it was not granted.

Mom's Guild Daily Report

Occupation: Ma-kun's one and only mommy
Name: Mamako Oosuki

Business Report:

We cleared the tower and reached the roof! Another goal met. Congratulations! Our road there was quite a challenge! A whole bunch of clones of me appeared and scared Ma-kun, and Amante's plan was so awful... I just couldn't let that stand, and I scolded the fake me's and Amante quite harshly.
Part of me regrets it, but I believe you should always say what you mean.

Other Notes:

This seems like the perfect opportunity to write about eggs! Temperature makes a big difference when it comes to an egg's freshness. Eggs keep better in the fridge or placed somewhere nice and cool. Generally speaking, if you can keep them below 60 degrees Fahrenheit, they should last about three weeks. They might last a little longer in the fridge (though opinions vary). Just a little FYI!

Member Comments:

Please stop talking about eggs...
The wounds are still fresh...

How many eggs are contaminated by salmonella again...?

Hey! No talking about germs here!
Masato's not the only one objecting!

Eggs should be safe raw as long as you keep them at the right temperature and eat them before the expiration date! But they're safer if you cook them!

Epilogue

The next morning, before sunrise, a single carriage set out from the coastal town.

It carried only one passenger: a female Fencer looking like she'd just taken a whiff of something foul—Amante.

"Like I said! I was at a disadvantage because of incomplete information! I didn't lose!"

She was shouting into a small magic circle in front of her.

"Which means you lost," a cold voice replied. *"You worthless scum."*

"Are you surpriiiised?" a sweet voice chimed in, drawing out their words. *"We aaaall know Amante's an iiiidiot."*

"I didn't lose!! And I'm not an idiot! You take that back!"

"I don't see the need. It's a fact."

"If you can't produce results, you can't gripe about what we saaaay. Stuuuupid."

"Grr... A-anyway, I'm headed back to you guys! Wait for me, okay?!"

"Whatever."

"I suppose we could wait, like...ten more seconds? Wow, I'm soooo nice! Byeee!"

With that uncooperative note, the magic circle vanished.

Amante was fuming.

"Ugh, they piss me off so much! This is all Mamako Oosuki's fault! ...I hate having to ask for help from the other three Lords, but that's the only way we're gonna take her down... Um, excuse me! How long till we reach the next town?"

The driver turned back, his smile failing to cover his irritation with her tone or the loud conversation.

"Well, let's see... We oughta reach Mahweh by evening..."

"Huh? Mahweh? But...but that's not the right place! Gah... I'm on the wrong carriage! Stop! Pull over, I'm getting out!"

"Can't, sorry. This carriage is fully automated, so it won't stop until we reach Mahweh."

"Huh? ...WHAAAAAT?!"

It was going to take Amante an unnecessarily long time to reach her destination.

The carriage raced on through the morning mist without stopping.

Today's breakfast at the Mom's Guild Hotel restaurant lounge was just a little bit special: egg over rice using freshly laid eggs.

You could find any of these ingredients at your local grocery store—that's how special this meal was.

"*Sigh...* The remains of what was once my wish... This is our reward...?"

Masato heaved a massive sigh as he cracked an egg over a small mixing bowl. The egg was so absurdly fresh that its contents gently oozed out, the luxuriant swell of the yolk ever so prominent. "GRAAAHH!!" Masato was going to pour every last ounce of his strength into beating that egg until it beat the resentment out of him, too!

Staring at Masato as he vented his frustrations was the party's female contingent. They were tucking into their meals quite peacefully.

"So, see, it turned out just like I'd said, right? And that's all 'cause of this precognition thing I've got as the Ultimate Sage, y'know."

"Sure, the wish turned out to be eggs, but it was Masato who actually made the wish, so your prediction wasn't *entirely* accurate. You should really tone down the vanity just a little."

"Mama, why did Masato wish for eggs?"

"Hee-hee. Why, that's because he wanted to give them to me as a present!"

"Personally, I feel that Masato should have just shouted 'Give me my mom's panties!' right then and there... But perhaps I'm just out of touch when it comes to children these days... Regardless, you were all able to prevent the enemy's wish from seeing the light of day. Now, then," said the person who had so quickly polished off Amante's portion of fresh eggs over rice—Shiraaase—before gently laying down her chopsticks and looking around at the group once more. "Everyone, I would like to applaud you for your efforts. Truly magnificent work."

"Yeah, thanks. At the end of it all, it was Mom's wish that got granted, and Amante escaped, so in all honesty I'm not particularly pleased with things... Also, what was up with this event anyway...?"

"Oh, come to think of it, you also weren't sure what was going on, right, Shiraaase?"

"Did you make any headway in your investigation?"

"I'm afraid I was unable to obtain any further information. I contacted each admin department several times with queries but never received a straight answer."

"Hmmm... Oh! Maybe someone is concealing the information on purpose?"

"That is certainly a possibility... An unexpected change to the event, the sudden appearance of a rebel group, and then that dark item... Given the lack of information regarding these developments, uncovering the truth behind it all will prove quite difficult... In any case, I shall continue on with my investigations... So what is it that you plan to do now, everyone?"

"Now what, huh...?"

What indeed. Any ideas? Masato looked around at his party for a volunteer.

Mamako raised her hand.

"Um, Ma-kun, what about staying in this town awhile?"

"Staying here? Why?"

"Well, it's such a lovely place! The view of the sea is delightful, the seafood is so good, and we know so many people here... Plus, we have a place to live!"

"Oh, right... Other than Porta, we're all registered as combatants, so it's pretty unusual for us to have a place to live like this."

"Normally, it's only possible for noncombatant players to create lodgings and live in them... Right, Porta?"

"That's right! But I'm a Traveling Merchant, which means I'm supposed to be traveling all the time, so it would pretty hard for me to have a shop of my own!"

"So this is a rare opportunity... Hmm... Then I guess we could stay awhile... I've got things I could do here, too..."

They might have cleared the tower, but it wasn't like they'd explored every inch of it. They'd skipped a bunch of floors. There might be items in there they hadn't found. Could be worth working their way slowly through it.

But as he considered this, a bell rang. "Is that—?" "Oh, the doorbell!" A magic one, at that.

Visitors? In the middle of breakfast?

They all headed to the entrance.

Pocchi and a crowd of adventurers were waiting there, dressed for construction work.

"Yo! Sorry to pop by so early! We got somethin' to show ya! Come with us!"

"Huh? Show us...what?"

Waved forward, they stepped outside and found a wagon parked in front with a huge stone monument on it.

There were letters carved into it, the largest of which read MOM'S GUILD, and next to that was the guild master's name, MAMAKO.

Then came Masato's name, about the same size as Mamako's, followed by a ton of footnotes:

*MAMAKO OOSUKI'S SON.

*OWNER OF THE HOLY SWORD OF THE HEAVENS.

*ABOUT 5' 6".

*HAS A SPECIAL POWER THAT LETS HIM KNOW IF SOMEONE IS A MOTHER.

And finally: *CALLS HIS MOTHER "MOM."

All these tidbits seemed entirely unnecessary to carve into anything.

"Uh... Pocchi... What is this...?"

"Awesome, right?! To celebrate you clearing the tower and to thank you for saving us, we're gonna put this up in the town square! ...And we gave you special treatment, Masato, completely on the house. Be grateful."

"Gee, thaaanks... Wait... Uh, what? The town square?"

"Yeah! Our moms have been talking you up all over town, so everyone knows about you now! There's even talk of holdin' some kinda ceremony!"

"W-wooow… You don't say…"

Everyone in town would know about them and come to stare at the monument.

*THIS BOY IS THE HERO, IN THE SENSE THAT HE WILLINGLY JOINED A GUILD CALLED MOM'S GUILD COMPOSED PRIMARILY OF MOMS.

They would read that footnote and then turn to look at Masato.

That's the hero? Mom's Guild? That takes courage, all right. He's his mother's hero!

Yep. There was no way he could live here.

"W-well, we've got a long journey ahead of us! …Time we got going!"

They had to leave now and never ever return to Thermo.

His mind made up, Masato immediately set to persuading Mamako.

"Right, Mom? We don't wanna stay here. Let's leave today! Okay!"

"Aw, but why so soon? You agreed to it just a moment ago."

"Y-yeah, I did, but… Uh…"

Should he admit he wanted to leave before rumors started spreading about him?

But then Mamako clapped her hands together.

"Oh, I understand! Ma-kun, you said you want to keep moving forward with Mommy! You want to go on adventures with Mommy!"

True, he had said that—back when they were facing Amante.

But that was mostly something he'd let slip because he wanted to take her on.

It wasn't that he *wanted* to be with his mom. It was that he'd managed to convince himself that the true adventure was surviving this *despite* having his mom there.

But it wasn't like it was completely wrong.

"Uh, sure, that's more or less right, I guess."

"I knew it! …Oh, I'm so happy to hear you actually say so, Ma-kun! It's like a dream come true! …But this is no time for dreaming, is it? I understand! Let's get ready to leave at once! I'll go tell the others!"

Mamako was practically sparkling.

All he had to do was agree with her and she was all smiles, running to tell the others, A Mother's Light shining as bright as her mood.

Masato stared after her.

"...What am I saying?"

He'd surprised himself by how positive he'd sounded. "Look, I'm just telling her what she wants to hear, okay? That's all." Excuses, excuses.

"But, well... This is our adventure, after all."

Masato let the words roll off his tongue, feeling like they weren't that bad.

Afterword

Thanks again. This is Dachima Inaka.

I've been blessed enough to get to volume three! This is entirely thanks to all of you. I want to extend my gratitude, and I hope you'll continue to support me for a long time to come.

This is a mom-centric series, and once again, there are lots of moms in it—sometimes so many moms I don't know how people will handle it...

But there is one thing I am clear on: This series is not intended to turn mothers into a laughingstock.

This series is (intended to be) a comedy, and part of the humor comes from exaggerated depictions of mom-like behavior. But at no point is it ever intended to mock the idea of mothers.

My hope is that the mothers depicted in this work will speak to your memories and experiences, remind you of that one-of-a-kind agony, and bring out a warm smile at the same time. That's the hope I have while writing this. There is always a danger I'll just dig up painful memories, but I hope you'll continue taking the bad with the good.

There are a few people I need to thank.

Iida Pochi. My editor, K. Everyone involved with publication and sales. Once again, I am grateful for all your help.

Also, Ai Kayano, who lent her voice to the marketing campaign, and the game developer Urufu, who created the *Mom* RPG. I feel I must mention you both, as I am so incredibly grateful. Thank you for all your hard work.

*   *   *

And finally, in place of my customary mom story is actually a message for my dad, since this volume is out in August.

Happy birthday! You were born, thus so was I, thus so was this book. You have my eternal gratitude.

Early summer 2017, Dachima Inaka

NEXT TIME

"Ma-kun, let's go to a casino together!"

Masato's party arrives in a town with a casino!

Looking forward to a brief respite (?), they get themselves
wrapped up in casino games...
...only to get carried away and sustain
devastating financial losses!!
And the only way to repay their debt...is for
Mamako to take a job as a bunny girl?!

Mom's looking to hit the jackpot in order to pay off their deficit!

A cutting-edge momcom adventure!
This time's the casino arc!

Do You Love Your Mom and Her Two-Hit Multi-Target Attacks?

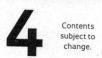

Contents
subject to
change.

ON SALE FALL 2019